THE

Storyteller's Beads

THE
Storyteller's Beads

▲ ▼ ▲ ▼ ▲ ▼ ▲ ▼ ▲ ▼ ▲ ▼ ▲ ▼ ▲ ▼ ▲ ▼

by Jane Kurtz

Gulliver Books

Harcourt Brace & Company

San Diego / New York / London

I would like to thank my older sister, Caroline, whose fluent Amharic and work in the Sudan were invaluable. Jim McKenzie, Libby Rankin, and Bob King guided and encouraged me through the early stages of the novel. I would have had a hard time imagining the details of Sahay's life without Frederick Gamst's ethnography of the Kemant. Richard Pankhurst's various writings always help me sort out the complexities of Ethiopian history. I am grateful to all the Beta-Israel who told their survival stories in such moving and compelling detail.

www.hmhbooks.com

Library of Congress Cataloging-in-Publication Data
Kurtz, Jane.
The storyteller's beads/Jane Kurtz,
p. cm.
Summary: During the political strife and famine of the 1980s, two Ethiopian girls, one Christian and the other Jewish and blind, struggle to overcome many difficulties, including their prejudices about each other, as they make the dangerous journey out of Ethiopia.

ISBN 978-0-15-201074-4 (hardcover)
ISBN 978-0-358-54628-3 (special markets paperback)

[1. Friendship—Fiction. 2. Prejudices—Fiction. 3. Blind—Fiction. 4. Physically handicapped—Fiction. 5. Ethiopia—Fiction.]
I. Title.
            PZ7.K9626St 1998
            [Fic]-dc2197-42312

Manufactured in the United States
DOC 10 9 8 7 6 5 4 3 2 1
4500807812

For Liz and Alison,
whose vision did so much
to bring this story to life

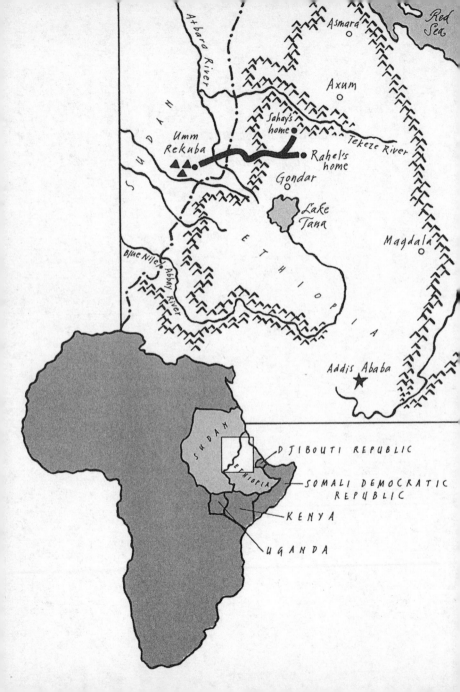

▲ ▼ ▲ ▼ ▲ ▼ ▲ ▼ ▲ ▼ ▲ ▼ ▲ ▼ ▲ ▼ ▲ ▼ ▲ ▼

PART 1

Sahay

▲ ▼ ▲ ▼ ▲ ▼ ▲ ▼ ▲ ▼ ▲ ▼ ▲ ▼ ▲ ▼ ▲

The Running

Sahay leaped up, tangling the thread she had been so carefully smoothing. The pounding of bare feet made her stomach chew on itself with fright. That sound! It was like the terrible day of running a year ago. . . . She pushed the thought away and stooped through the doorway of the house, still clutching the spindle from her spinning.

The fields in front of the house were too brown for the twelfth month, Nahase. By this time, the gray green barley should look like light cotton cloth blowing in the mountain winds. But this year—the year of Sahay's sadness—the rains had not fallen to wet the fields.

The man running toward Sahay through the fields was her uncle. Sahay's insides began to beat so loudly in her ears that she felt as if she must be running, too. She dropped the spindle to the ground, not noticing that the dust curled up to make the white thread brown.

"Hurry." Her uncle was panting so hard that the words came out in gasps. "We must leave this place."

Sahay tried to speak, but her throat felt choked and dry, and no words came out. She turned back, blindly, and stooped through the doorway.

The hot, peppery smell of supper filled the *tukul*. In the darkest back part of the house, the *saweh* simmered in a pot that sat on three stones over the fire. But Sahay could not think of hunger now.

Her uncle ducked through the door after her. He picked up the traveling basket and pushed it into her hands. It was the basket he used to carry his food when he went to the faraway Gondar *markato*. "Put the meal in this." He rushed to where his walking stick leaned against the wall.

Sahay knelt, trembling. The fire popped and a spark flew at her. She brushed it away. Once, when she and her mother were cooking, Sahay had asked, "Why do we always cook where it is so dark?"

Her mother didn't like Sahay to ask questions. But that day she did answer. "So the evil eye of a stranger cannot fall on our food."

"But no stranger ever comes here."

Her mother had poured the *arah* on the griddle, and they watched it start to bubble. "May it always be so," she had said.

It was not always so. As the Red Terror that started in the south spread, the strangers came: first *shiftas,* thieves who before had stolen only from travelers on the roads. Next, as war and famine seized the lands to the north, came soldiers and people looking for new lands.

"Let them take Falasha lands—not ours," Sahay's father had shouted then. "The Falasha were not even allowed to own land until these new, evil times."

Her uncle had agreed. "Let the strangers from the north take Falasha land." But the strangers tried to take everybody's land.

Don't think about that now. Sahay laid the *arah* in the bottom of the basket, scooped the *saweh* onto it, and then closed the basket. Her fingers shook on the straps she knew so well. For the same reason she had been taught to cook in the back of the house, she had also been taught not to let strangers see the food the family carried.

Aii! Her mother had been right about evil strangers. She put her hand to her mouth to stop the sound that burst out.

Her uncle rushed over and shook her gently. "Quickly," he said. "Put some grain and dried meat into a cloth and tie it tightly. I do not know how many days we will have to travel."

Many days? Sahay had never slept any place except in these beds her father had made from trees and strips of leather. Except for the pots and iron things made by Falashas, everything in this house had been made by her mother and father.

Her uncle was tying some coins into a cloth. "Hurry," he said again.

Sahay scooped up a handful of grain, spilling a little through her shaking fingers. A chicken ran up and pecked at it. Most of the chickens had been eaten or sold, but a few were still alive. "Shall we take the chickens?" she asked. It was the first time she had spoken since her uncle came home, and her voice sounded strange to her.

"We have no time to run after chickens." Her uncle grabbed his walking stick. "I have a little money and two *gahbis* for warmth. Give me the basket of food and see if you can find any more. I'm going to make sure the way of our path is safe. Be ready to leave when I return."

Sahay stared after him. Where could they possibly go? Were there other of her people, the Kemant, living in a safer place, a place strangers hadn't found yet? Her grandfather had told her of visiting the strong stone castles at Gondar. Right now, she would like to be inside some place strong and made of stone.

Sahay spread a cloth and added what little dried meat they had left from when her father had butchered one of the last cows more than a year ago. Then she scooped a handful of chickpeas from a storage basket. How much food did they need? When the strangers came before, it took all of the Kemant people around this area a whole day to drive them off. One long day of fighting. This time, it might take even longer. How long?

Sahay filled the cloth with chickpeas and knotted it tightly. Part of her wanted to cry out that she did not want to go, did not want to leave this house where she had always lived. But another part was as dried up as the dried peas. *What does this house matter?* that part whispered. *Now that your mother and father are not here, anyway?*

She ran to her father's walking stick beside the door. Whenever he was going a long distance, he used to take his walking stick. She would look at him and think how strong and bold he looked standing at the door. "Father, may your walking stick give me some of your strength," she said aloud. But she did not feel strong and bold as she stepped out into the cool evening air.

The light was very dim now. It was the time they should have been lighting the beeswax candle that leaned out from the pole in the center of the *tukul.* Sahay could barely see the animal huts, empty because the animals had either died from hunger or been sold to buy food. Beyond the huts were the dark shapes of the eucalyptus trees her grandfather had planted for her and her cousins.

Sahay shivered and listened carefully. All she could hear were the small animals and birds that call at dusk.

Then her uncle was standing beside her with his walking stick in his hand. "We will do well," he said, "if we leave now." He started off quickly without looking at the house, so Sahay did not look back either. She followed him down the path, trying not to look over her shoulder to see what might be coming behind, keeping her eyes on the white of his *gahbi* as the dark pressed down.

▲ ▼ ▲ ▼ ▲ ▼ ▲ ▼ ▲ ▼ ▲ ▼ ▲ ▼ ▲

Night Escape

At first, the path was smooth under Sahay's bare feet. With the stick to help her find a rhythm, she walked with quick sureness, the way she might walk down to the stream to get water. But the fear, pounding on her as though she were a drum, told her this night was different.

The ground was warm—too warm. By this time, the potatoes should have sprouted flowers and the dark green shoots of the oil seed plants should have grown halfway to her knees instead of lying dry and shriveled. When Sahay was a child and people had said, "Let your enemies be like dust," she had hardly known what dust meant.

In those happy days, Sahay and her cousins had run along this path to the sacred groves, hopping around in the cool morning air, until her grandmother would say, "Children and rain make me happy even when they annoy." If she listened now, Sahay could almost imagine she heard the solemn music of the *bagana,* far-off, as the priest plucked its strings. At the place where the trees grew thick, another priest would be sprinkling milk and honey on the sacred ground and on the trees. When it was time, the whole community would walk in among the trees. Sahay always knew, in those days, where she belonged and what people she belonged with. Now, though the path hadn't changed, she didn't know where she belonged or where she was going.

Suddenly, her uncle stopped beside a pile of stones stacked by the road. Even in the dim light, Sahay could see that the stones were stained black from the lumps of butter people had left as offerings.

"Untie your food bag," her uncle whispered, as he pulled at the top of his own bag.

When the bags were open, he put a handful of grain in front of the stones and a few chickpeas on top of the grain. Then he said, "We offer thanks that we reached this place safely. May God allow us to be successful in the trip we are about to take."

Sahay remembered this prayer from the trips to the grove, but now it was hushed and hurried. She wanted to stay by the stones. Perhaps God would send some kind of answer. Perhaps her mother or father or grandmother would speak. But her uncle pulled her hand. "Come, Sahay."

Now the path was no longer familiar, and Sahay stared into the darkness trying to figure out where they were, where they might be going. Her uncle would know a place. He was the one her father had always sent to the Gondar *markato* to buy honey, bars of salt, and the tools that only Falashas could make because only Falashas worked with iron. Her uncle liked the travels and he would come back with his face lively from the things he had seen. Right now, she wished she could hold the back of her uncle's *gahbi*. But he was walking too fast. "Wait," she whispered, but he didn't hear.

She pulled her own *gahbi* tight around her chin. If only she could go back. Back to the time before the Red Terror.

How had the Red Terror come north from the faraway capital of Addis Ababa? How had it caught up with her? She remembered being a young child huddled by the fire, listening to the adults talk of the Red Terror. They talked of the Amhara king of kings Haile Selassie, last in a long line of Amhara kings, who was pulled from his throne by a military committee.

But she had never understood what faraway Amhara kings or military committees had to do with her people here in the north. Most of her people, though they spoke Amharic, stayed in their own communities, separate from the Amhara, who had ruled Ethiopia for so long that only the old stories held the memories of any other times.

Before the Red Terror came to her family, everything was good. If she or her cousins had misbehaved, the adults didn't slap them but only said, "A hyena will get you" or, sometimes, "A stranger will harm you." But no strangers came. Only other Kemant came to the house. Then her mother would send Sahay to get food and drink for them, and water to wash their feet. "They are our people," her mother would say.

Thinking about her mother now made Sahay sick with sadness. "Uncle," she whispered. She tried to grab his *gahbi*, but she couldn't reach it. Tiredness rushed over her. She stumbled and almost fell.

"Sahay." Her uncle turned around to look at her. "Let's rest and eat."

They sat by the side of the path, and Sahay's uncle untied the food basket. The *arah* and *saweh* were hardly warm anymore, but Sahay was glad to touch something she had prepared before she knew anything of this night's travels. For a moment, with the sour and hot taste of the food resting in her mouth, she felt that she would somehow make it through this journey, wherever they were going, as she had survived so much else.

Then, from out of the darkness, came the *oop-oop-oop* of a hyena. Sahay shivered and dropped the food she was eating.

Her uncle looked up. "*Ayezosh*. Have courage. Hyenas eat almost nothing except animals that other animals have killed."

Sahay remembered the few times she had seen a

hyena's twisted body and shining eyes when it came too close to the house at night. She began to pack the food, quickly. "Let's go on," she said.

"Yes," her uncle said softly. "We should go."

As they walked, the moon came up. Her uncle said, "At least we will have light. But we must be quiet. We are in more danger from other human beings than from any animal."

Sahay remembered how the adults had talked of *shiftas* who—from as far back as anyone could remember—would hide in the wild places and attack and rob people. At those times, safe by the fire with her own family, she had never imagined she would be out in the wilds herself at night. She hit her foot on a stone and held her mouth to keep from crying out.

Step. Step. Step. Sahay was so tired, she was nearly walking in her sleep. Suddenly, she heard a donkey's foolish laughter and saw a cluster of *tukuls* up ahead. Their roofs looked strange in the moonlight.

"A Falasha village," her uncle whispered.

Falasha! The very word meant alien stranger. Many times Sahay had heard about Falasha who turned themselves into hyenas and ran through the countryside at night. People said if a Falasha walked on a person's land, grass and crops would never grow there again.

"This road will be smoother for a while," her uncle said. "It will let us walk far tonight."

"Will it take us quickly from the Falasha village?"

Sahay held tight to her walking stick and wondered if she could swing it as a weapon if she needed to. "Do you think one of them might turn himself into a hyena and follow us?"

Her uncle laughed softly in the dark. "I have always bought the iron parts for my plow and my hoes from this village. For myself, I do not put much faith in the old stories about hyenas and *budas*."

Sahay shook her head. Her uncle could say what he wanted. Too many times, she had heard a Falasha called *buda*, a person with an evil eye. How could it not be true?

By the light of the moon, the trees by the side of the road looked like twisted men. *Ayezosh,* Sahay whispered to herself. She felt far from anything like courage. But somehow she had found courage to escape into the hills on that terrible day of running when the shouting came. Somehow she had found the little cave she and her cousins used to hide in when they were children. But she . . . No. She held her father's walking stick more tightly and whispered to herself that she would clout a hyena on the nose if it came near.

After so many miles that Sahay thought she would just lie down and sleep on the road, her uncle finally said, "We'll stop here by this stream for the night. Among those big rocks over there, we can find a hidden place to sleep."

Sahay wrapped herself in her *gahbi* and lay on the rough ground beside her uncle. The creaking of night bugs was peaceful, and she was so tired . . . so tired. *If a Falasha hyena comes and carries me off in the night,* she thought in her half sleep, *at least I will not have to walk anymore.* Sleepiness made her bold enough to ask, "When will we go back home?"

Her uncle did not say anything. Then he whispered, "It could be many years before we return."

Sahay was suddenly awake. She felt as if she had been slapped. *"Years?"*

Her uncle shifted on the hard ground and sighed. "When I was plowing, some Kemant from a place a little to the north came running. They said a large group of armed men were moving southward, looking for land to grab. The men had already seized the fields of these Kemant and killed others who resisted. What could I do to defend my land? I do not even have a gun. I sold what land I had left to one of our neighbors who has a gun." He was silent for a moment. Then he said, "Sahay, I must find a safe place for you. You are our family's only hope for the future."

Her uncle had sold their home? Sahay wanted to put back her head and howl as dogs did. The night breeze rippled the edge of her *gahbi,* and the memory of her mother's hands against her face washed over her, making her dizzy with longing. She stuffed her *gahbi* into her mouth so no one would hear her if she whimpered aloud. Finally she let tiredness cover her.

A strange bird called out from the darkness, then sleep came.

That night, Sahay dreamed her father was plowing. The kites with their red wings were soaring above him, and little blue-green birds darted around the fields. Sahay and her mother followed behind the plow, tossing tiny seeds into the air. In the dream, the seeds flew up and up, and she stood, looking into the sky, watching the kites eat those seeds meant for her family, who would have no grain, no bread, nothing to eat.

▲ ▼ ▲ ▼ ▲ ▼ ▲ ▼ ▲ ▼ ▲ ▼ ▲ ▼ ▲ ▼ ▲ ▼

PART 2

Rahel

▲ ▼ ▲ ▼ ▲ ▼ ▲ ▼ ▲ ▼ ▲ ▼ ▲ ▼ ▲

The Whispering

Rahel knelt and felt for the grinding stone. She placed her handful of grain on the flat rock and began to push the grinding stone against it. This was the first job her grandmother had taught her after Rahel woke from the long illness a few years ago and saw only darkness when she held her hand in front of her face. She had heard the whispers, then, that she would be of no use to anyone. "Foolish talk," her grandmother had said, guiding Rahel's hands to the stone.

Backward and forward, over and over. The stone made a nice scraping sound. But Rahel frowned anyway. This morning when she had put her hand into the grain bin, her fingers had touched the bottom.

After she had ground the grain into coarse flour, Rahel sat back. The flat rock the family used as a grindstone was set against the outside wall of the *tukul,* where the overhanging grass roof would protect it from rain. But this year, the grindstone might as well have been in the middle of the yard. This year, the little rains had not come, and now the big rains did not seem to be coming either.

"My stomach is aching with fear that we will have nothing to eat," she had said to Grandmother just last night.

"We will eat," Grandmother had said. "When the grain is gone, we'll live on cabbage. It has happened before."

Rahel had not said that even the cabbages were like dried leaves.

Rahel got up and let her feet find the way to the edge of the swept yard and then a little farther, to the tree that she called Judge Deborah's tree. She imagined that the breeze was bringing the smell of Tekemt, the month of harvest. She did not have to look at the ugly dry hillsides her grandmother described to her. No, she could see them green, with bright yellow daisies and blue flax blossoms.

Girls' voices on the path startled her. For a moment she wanted to run. Instead, she stood absolutely still, even willing the breeze to not move one hair on her head. She could not see the girls. It was easy to pretend they could not see her.

From their footsteps, she could tell that they were almost past when one of them did see her. Their voices drifted back.

"What? What is it?"

"No one. Just the blind Falasha girl."

No one. Rahel flicked her *shamma* around her and walked back to the house. No, she was *not* a blind Falasha girl. She was Deborah—great judge of the children of Israel—who had just finished sitting under her tree and giving out wisdom. The sun was blessing her face; the chickens were clucking in amazement as she walked by them. "Come, chicken," she said, as she stooped to scoop the flour from the stone. "Tell me news of yourself." The hen squawked, and she laughed.

Rahel ducked inside, into the coolness. The house said *injera, injera* this morning. She could hear the *glub-glub* sound of her mother stirring the batter. Her grandmother was probably sitting in the corner spinning. Rahel liked to put her fingers in the cotton web and feel the fineness of the thread.

"Mama," Rahel whispered. "The grain is almost gone."

She listened to her mother sniffing the batter. It must have the right sour smell before it would make good bread. There was a rustling, and then a coin was pressed into her hand.

"Go with your grandmother to the market," her mother said. "This last coin will buy a little more grain."

Rahel took the coin but she did not move. "Your brother is selling hoes at the *markato*," Rahel's mother went on. "If he sells some iron things, there will be more coins."

Questions tapped at Rahel's head. If the farmers did not have grain to sell, they would also have no money. Who would buy the hoes? Who would buy the cloth her father wove? But when she opened her mouth, her mother said, "Remember. It is not polite for children to question their elders."

So, with her fingers curled among the strong fingers of her grandmother, Rahel walked quickly toward the village, feeling the dust on her bare feet. But she still wondered: *How can people live without food or money?*

Perhaps the prophet Elias would come, as he had come to a widow whose food had all run out. Rahel imagined that she was the widow, gathering sticks for her fire. She imagined the prophet Elias calling out to her, "Would you bring me a little water and a piece of bread?"

Rahel pretended she was looking sadly at the prophet in his white robes. "I have only a handful of flour and a little oil. I'm going to make a piece of bread for myself and my son. We will eat it, and then our last food will be gone and we will die."

But the story had a good ending. The widow made bread for the prophet, instead. And the jar of flour was never used up, and the jug of oil never ran dry, until the Lord gave rain on the land. What a luxury it would be to plunge her fingers into a jar of flour as soft as fine cloth.

When the noise of the *markato* reached her ears,

Rahel's feet slowed. If a girl who was Beta-Israel did anything to make the children of the village angry, they would not only call her Falasha but—worse—a *buda* with evil magic power. They might even throw stones.

Things were bad in the village these days. Someone had set the roof of the prayer house on fire twice, and the Beta-Israel men had to rush to put it out. Rahel pretended she was a small weasel, slipping past the legs of the people on their way to the *markato*. She hoped her grandmother was doing the same so they would not be noticed.

As they neared the *markato*, Rahel could smell the bright spices, heaped on trays, and the butter, wrapped in green leaves. The smell of honey made her think of the round cakes of yellow beeswax. Best of all at the *markato* were the glass beads in neat piles that her grandmother sometimes guided her fingers to. Rahel could have touched the silky beads all day. She thought of asking Grandmother to take her there, but instead, she said, "Is my brother in his usual place?"

"He is," her grandmother said, "and, praise God, he's smiling." Rahel moved quickly toward where she knew the Beta-Israel blacksmiths were selling iron tools. She picked her way along the edge of the pottery area, among the jugs and cups, water pots, cooking pots, and pitchers. How angry her brother, Dawit, would be if she broke something. Lately, since he had come back from Addis Ababa, he had seemed always angry.

When she felt Dawit's hand on her arm, Rahel held out the coin. "It's for grain. It's the last one."

She touched Dawit's face as he took the coin, but his forehead did not wrinkle in anger. Perhaps he looked, at this moment, the way he used to look when the two of them would take the cattle to find grass each day, when she would play her flute out on the hillsides and he would lie back and dream. He had not seemed that happy for at least a year, thirteen months.

"Are you selling any of the iron things?"

"Some." His voice sounded calm and cheerful. "But the prices are not good." Rahel wanted to ask him what would happen when the grain was completely gone. When they used to run together after the cattle, she could have asked. Now she wouldn't dare. After the Beta-Israel schools were closed, her brother had been sent to live with relatives and go to high school in Addis Ababa. He had returned angry, so angry he even talked back to their father. So now Rahel said nothing. She turned and made her way back to Grandmother, putting her feet down with care to not trample the pottery.

Just as Rahel felt Grandmother's hand, she stopped. Something seemed to be happening in the *markato*. Was it her imagination, or did she hear a whisper run from neighbor to neighbor? "Get ready. It's time. It's time."

When she shut out all the other babbling sounds, Rahel could hear her father. She knew he would be standing under the big tree talking with other Beta-Israel men. *Get ready for what?* she wanted to ask. *Time for what?* When her grandmother stopped to greet some of the other women, Rahel let go of Grandmother's hand and slipped through the crowd until she felt the tree trunk against her hand.

"It is time," she heard her father say softly. "The elders have always said our people came to Ethiopia from the west and someday must go back by the west. The message has come..." His voice became so low that Rahel could not hear the words.

The babble of voices from the *markato* mixed with the wind in the branches of the tree. Then high above in the sky, Rahel heard another sound. A machine of the sky.

Late that night, Rahel moaned in her sleep. Her grandmother, lying nearby, reached out with a soft sound.

Rahel sat up. "I dreamed we were leaving," she whispered.

"Ah," Grandmother said. *"Shh-shhh-shhh."* Rahel smelled the eucalyptus stick that Grandmother broke, then heard the fire lick the wood. "Go back to sleep and to new dreams."

"But I think we are leaving." Shivers ran up Rahel's arms. "I heard Father say so."

She heard her grandmother pick up the spindle. Even in the darkness, it was possible to pull a thin thread from the ball of cotton and smooth out the lumps. When the cotton was spun, her father would weave it into *shamma* cloth for someone to wear. But how could her father carry a big, heavy loom if they left this place?

Finally, Grandmother said, "Perhaps the time has come. The corn we planted in the garden did not come up this year. They say there is terrible hunger farther north."

Rahel put her chin on her knee and let Grandmother's voice fall over her like the web of cotton. Grandmother had taught her so much. After the eye sickness, Grandmother had been like God teaching Adam and Eve, the first people. She had taught Rahel to name with her fingers everything that she had once named with her eyes.

Grandmother went on. "Today I saw one of those machines of the air far above me in the sky. The machines will bring rain—a rain of fire—on our village."

"I heard the machine," Rahel said. "But there was only one."

"As our people say, 'One stone is enough against fifty clay pots.'"

"To leave our home is also dangerous," Rahel argued. Grandmother, who was a wise elder and stubborn about speaking her own mind, would put up with a little arguing.

"Yes," Grandmother said. "To leave home is always dangerous. But sometimes to stay can be even more dangerous. I have heard that soldiers come into the villages to take young men to fight in the war to the north."

They sat in silence. Outside, something scratched in the dirt. A dog? Or was it a hyena, or a leopard? Rahel shivered. "Dawit is a young man now," she said. She imagined the soldiers bursting into their *tukul,* Dawit scrambling to hide. Where? Behind a water jug?

Grandmother said nothing, but Rahel heard her hands, pulling the thread.

Rahel listened for the sound of Dawit's breathing. All these months when he seemed so angry, he must have been worried. No wonder he was happy today. The murmur that had rippled through the Beta-Israel in the *markato* had reached his ears, too. She shivered again and whispered, "I have heard stories of things that happen in the dark."

"Stories," Grandmother said. "Ah yes. But you, my small lover of stories, will also remember the stories that give courage. Do you remember the story I have told you about our beautiful Queen Yehudit?"

Rahel lay back. She wrapped her blanket tight

around her and stretched out her fingers to the fire, where the eucalyptus branch was no longer crackling. "Tell me again."

"Long, long ago," Grandmother began, "the mighty kingdom of Axum stood in the north, full of palaces, churches, and tall monuments."

Rahel closed her eyes and let the story curl around her.

"The time came when the people of the kingdom of Axum began to push south into the lands of other people. Our people. For many years, they pushed. Our people did not push back. But Queen Yehudit was a very brave woman, they say, and when the time came, she rose up. She left her home and led her people against the mighty city of Axum. And the mighty city fell."

As Grandmother's voice went on, Rahel saw Queen Yehudit in her mind. The queen, crouched on a steaming horse, thundered into the mighty city of Axum, triumphant and strong. *Where did she get the courage?* "If only there were a river of courage," Rahel whispered. "I would bend down, cup the water in my hand, and drink."

▲ ▼ ▲ ▼ ▲ ▼ ▲ ▼ ▲ ▼ ▲ ▼ ▲ ▼ ▲ ▼ ▲

Secret Meeting

Rahel woke to a house that said *buna, buna*. Her mother must be roasting beans over the fire. The bold coffee smell scattered the night terrors and made the murmuring in the marketplace seem like a dream.

Grandmother gave a little groan. "This will be a day of hard work," she said, as she pressed a few grains of parched wheat into Rahel's hand. Rahel ate the kernels, one by one. What was different about today? Every day was a day of hard work. Food always needed to be made and clothes washed, firewood found and water carried.

As if Grandmother had heard her thoughts, she said, "Today we will make pottery. If God wills it, a new line of pots will be drying in front of the house by evening."

Rahel smiled. She liked to imagine the new pots with their fat, sleek bellies and thin necks.

"This day!" Mother's voice was worried and scolding. "It has filled itself with things to do."

Rahel's smile drained away. *Things for leaving?* Rahel wanted to ask. She felt Grandmother's hand on her wrists, lifting her hands. "These hands," Grandmother said, "and my hands are strong enough to do the pottery today."

Rahel waited until they were outside to ask, "Why should we make pottery if we are leaving?"

For a time Grandmother did not answer. Instead, she guided Rahel to the place where the mud was smooth and cool as water. Rahel dug her fingers in, making three piles. She knew how the piles would look: one red, one sandy, one black. Grandmother would be adding pieces of broken pots.

It was time to carry water from the stream, balancing it in pots on their heads. Whenever she carried the water, Rahel liked to act as if she were the Rahel she was named after, the Rahel from the story in the Books of Moses. Today she was especially glad for the pretending that took her thoughts from all her questions. Imagining that she was the Rahel in the story, she swayed gracefully up the path. Soon Yakob would see her and think she was wonderful—so wonderful that he would work seven long years to be able to marry her.

But at the end of the seven long years, Rahel's father would trick Yakob and give him Leah, Rahel's older sister, instead. So Yakob would have to work another seven long years before he got to marry Rahel. How angry the other Rahel must have felt, waiting for fourteen years because of her unfair father.

Grandmother's arm told her it was time to stop. Water splashed onto the clay and onto her bare feet. Rahel knelt and began to knead. Suddenly, Grandmother spoke. "Journeys take money. In three days when these pots are dry, we will fire them. Then they can be sold at the *markato*. The money will be useful on your trip."

Rahel stopped kneading. What had Grandmother said?

"Do not stop working, Rahel. The work will not do itself."

Rahel tried to think. *Your trip?* What, exactly, had Grandmother said last night? Had she agreed they were leaving? Had she said they might not? For a moment, Rahel didn't hear anything, even the chicken that was scratching beside her. A sudden jolt of fear rattled through her. It was as if she were the only person left in the whole world. She had felt this once before, waking from the sickness, opening her eyes and seeing only darkness.

They wouldn't really go and leave me all alone, though, would they? Rahel thought. To calm herself she listened for the clunk of her father's loom beside the *tukul*. Her father often sat there weaving cotton into cloth, his feet in a hole he had dug under the loom. No. No familiar loom sounds. Then with a rush of relief, she heard her grandmother dip something—probably a corncob—into water and begin to polish a pot. The familiar sounds brought Rahel back to herself. She began to push and fold the clay.

Grandmother finally spoke. "I am too old for the road. The path to Zion is hard, and they say some will not make it. I have lived in this house all my life, and this is where I will stay."

Rahel moaned and reached out for Grandmother. Grandmother got to her feet, resting her hands briefly on Rahel's head. "Today my old hands feel weak, and the clay says *imbi*—'I refuse.' I will let the clay rest and will go to find wood to fire these pots. You keep kneading."

Rahel wanted to call out, "No, come back. Tell me more," but she made herself keep touching the warm, wet clay. Everything inside was quivering. She longed to jump up and run after the sound of Grandmother's footsteps.

If only she could go along and help search for the wood. She was no longer good for that job. Though she could spin, help make the pottery, and hold her aunts' babies when they were quarrelsome, she missed going to the groves of trees on the hillsides, seeing the way the wind blew their branches and spread the smell of eucalyptus everywhere. She missed the little cups that fell from the trees that she and her friends would sip water from, when they were young girls, pretending it was *buna*.

Rahel pulled a wooden flute from the bag at her waist and rocked a little as she made the sound of the wind in the trees. The music comforted her a bit.

That evening seemed as if it might be any evening. Grandmother and Mother cooked *injera* on a griddle balanced on three rocks over the cook fire. There was no meat for the *wat,* but Rahel liked the way the spicy lentil stew exploded in her mouth.

Suddenly, Father said, "Tonight is a secret meeting for all the Beta-Israel who live in and around this village. We will all go."

Silence followed Father's words. Then Dawit let out a kind of shout.

"Did you leave your wits behind you in the city?" Father growled. "A secret meeting must be held in quiet." Rahel felt as if she had swallowed one of the clay pots.

As they went down the path toward the village, Rahel groped for Grandmother's hand. Her feet knew this path, but at night everything was different. That sound was probably a *shifta* rustling the bushes, ready to jump out and rob them. And was that panting a hyena or a leopard, crouched beyond the next bend? She tried not to think about the stories she had heard of spirits who came out at night. What did spirits sound like?

Long ago, before her illness, she had once been

scurrying beside Grandmother because darkness had caught them when they were still out on the foot-path. Holding on to Grandmother's dress so the dark could not reach out its hands and grab her, Rahel had looked up to see stars—platters and platters of stars—blazing at her, so fat and startling that she had screamed. Grandmother had scooped her up and comforted her with a soft clicking sound, saying, "Rahel, God showed these same stars to Abraham and said that Abraham and Sara's children would number more than the stars. And see? We are the children of Abraham." Rahel wished she were still small enough for Grandmother to pick her up and comfort her as she had done that night.

Finally, a thin stream of sound told Rahel they were near the village. The Beta-Israel usually stayed to their own part of the village, only having contact with the other villagers at the *markato* or when they happened to meet along the path. Sometimes when Rahel was young, she trembled after those chance meetings and touched her dress, which suddenly felt so ragged. "Rahel!" her grandmother would say. "Amhara and Tigrean people might own land and have money. But you are a child of Abraham and Sara. You are one of God's chosen people."

Rahel imagined the moonlight on the prayer house, a *tukul,* like her own home only bigger, with the star of David on top of the grass roof. As Grandmother guided her inside, she could tell from the low voices that the prayer house was already filled with people—men on one side, women on the other. When Grandmother let go of her hand, Rahel found her way to one of the mud walls and curled there, listening to the soft chatter of younger children.

After a few moments, Rahel heard the drum and the rhythm of feet and wooden prayer sticks on the earthen floor. A *kes* began to recite the story of the Exodus, when Moses led the children of Israel out of Egypt and to their own promised land. Rahel almost forgot she was at a secret meeting. Instead, she imagined that it was the holiday of Fasika, when people told this exodus story over and over in all its detail. She had always loved when it was time to act out the story, pretending that she could hear Moses up ahead. Moses would lift his walking stick so the Red Sea could slide into two parts and let the children of Israel through. But the Egyptians who were chasing them would be swallowed up. She loved the prayer at the end of the Fasika festival, to God "who brought us to this day and did not forget us."

Tonight when the story was finished, one of the older men spoke the words Rahel had heard so many times. "We came from Jerusalem, and one day we will return to Jerusalem."

"In Jerusalem," another of the older men said, "we will be dressed in white. We will pray all day. I've heard there is a road through the desert that will take us to Jerusalem."

"But the way to Jerusalem will be hard," the first answered.

A younger man spoke up. "How can we leave our lands?"

"How many of us have land?" Rahel's father asked sharply. "As the Amhara say, 'The sky has no pillar and the Falasha has no land.' "

"We came from Jerusalem," the first elder said again. "And it is written in our holy books that one day we will return to Jerusalem. The day has now come."

Rahel's stomach twisted. Above her head, she heard the clucking of a chicken, as if the chicken agreed. Who would take care of the chickens if everybody left?

She was not surprised to hear Grandmother speak. Grandmother was a *baaltet,* one of the wise older women, and people would listen when she spoke. "Our people came on foot through the Sudan," Grandmother said. "We will return on foot through the Sudan." Even though the words were familiar to Rahel, this time she felt comfort seep into her because Grandmother said *we.*

The talk went on about how the last Ethiopian king had been thrown out by a military committee. How under the new government, the Beta-Israel had finally been given land. But that land was often worn out and full of rocks, and the old landlords came back to burn houses and chase the Beta-Israel away. Rahel heard again the words *Red Terror* and *White Terror*.

Whatever terrors came along, her people were caught in the middle of them. There was never enough money. Some years there was food and some years there was no food. But this year, something was different. This year, on top of everything being so hard, these strange whispers had come to the *markato*. Had *aliyah*—the time of leaving talked about in the old stories—really come? The question bounced from one person to the next.

"Maybe we are all dreaming." A man's loud voice rained down on everybody in the meeting. "Who knows what else besides sickness waits when we leave our mountains? We may all die before we reach the Sudan."

Silence spread over the room. Then Rahel heard a voice that didn't sound familiar to her—a soft voice, a voice of hidden places. "I have been to the Sudan," the voice said. "Not all will make it. But we can hire a guide to take us down the mountains. From there, we can go to Jerusalem."

Many men began to talk at once. Finally, a *kes* told the Exodus story again, stopping in places to say the familiar prayers. "Show us the light of your praise, Lord, deliver us because of your name, and redeem us."

The talk was like flies buzzing. Rahel pulled her *shamma* around her ears and imagined herself one of the children of Israel, huddled in the dark just before the Exodus, waiting for the Angel of Death to pass over. People must have been scared—but excited, too. Maybe it would be exciting to set off for Jerusalem, away from hunger and terror. But *not* without Grandmother.

▲ ▼ ▲ ▼ ▲ ▼ ▲ ▼ ▲ ▼ ▲ ▼ ▲ ▼ ▲ ▼

The Journey

▲ ▼ ▲ ▼ ▲ ▼ ▲ ▼ ▲ ▼ ▲ ▼ ▲ ▼ ▲

Buda

Before it was light, Sahay felt her uncle's hand on her shoulder and heard his whisper. "How did you spend the night?"

For a moment, she felt comfortable and warm. In the darkness, she imagined it was one of the good years when the grains, potatoes, garlic, onions, and red peppers were all growing well, and she was getting up before the sun came into the sky to help her mother with work around the house before going out to the fields.

But then the memories rushed back, and she twisted on the hard ground. "I don't think I have the strength to go on," she said.

"Sahay." Her uncle's voice was firm. "You were always a stubborn girl. Remember how we used to scold you and Waldu when you ran off in the middle of your work? You must use that same stubbornness, in Waldu's memory."

Her uncle hardly ever said Waldu's name. The shock of hearing it now made Sahay angry, and she pushed away the handful of grain her uncle held out to her.

Light was just beginning to seep into the sky. Sahay sat up and listened to the sound of running water. The stream was not far from where she had slept. Was this the same stream she had scooped water from for so many years?

As she washed her face, Sahay hoped the icy water she was touching had run by her house yesterday. The cold water made her calm again. Why be angry with her uncle? She would save her anger in case she ever had the chance to spit in the face of the strangers who had ruined everything.

She picked up her father's walking stick. "We'll use the path for now," her uncle said. "But you must be ready to run to the side and hide. I'm sure we will meet some people going to one of the faraway *markatos,* but one can't know who else will come down this path."

In happier times, Sahay had loved going to her own village *markato*—cotton from the lowlands, salt from the Danakil desert, pottery made by Falasha women. Her mother would laugh and chatter with relatives, while Sahay stared with big eyes at the bangles and beads, the beautiful cloth woven by Falasha weavers. She had dreamed of how wonderful the big Gondar *markato* must be, and once, when Waldu got to go along with his father, had even said to her mother, "I want to go, too."

"Hush," her mother had said. "You don't know the dangers a person can meet on the road." Sahay felt the same shiver of fear now that she had felt then—but she also smiled a little to remember what a stubborn child she had been, how she had turned away and whispered to herself, "I still want to go someday."

In the morning light, her fears of hyenas and *budas* seemed far away. The juniper and wild fig trees no longer looked frightening. When they came around a curve in the path, an antelope scrambled on graceful legs to get out of their way. True, Sahay's feet were sore. But she sang a soft song and imagined that she was going to the Gondar *markato* with her uncle and Waldu after all.

For just a moment, she was even almost glad to be free of the house with all its terrible memories. Perhaps the land where they were going would have wonderful *markatos* with bangles and beads and beautifully embroidered *shammas* and delicious food. Perhaps they would live in a big house with a stream running right by the door so she would never have to carry heavy pots of water for many, many steps. Perhaps strangers would never again come to ruin people's lives. Perhaps.

As the sun climbed in the sky, Sahay and her uncle

began to overtake other travelers. Sahay glanced at them, but they did not look like soldiers, land grabbers, or *shiftas*. Most carried loads of wood or grain. Her uncle and the other people called out the customary greetings to one another. "How have you passed the night?"

"Thanks be to God, I am well. How are you?"

"Thanks be to God, I am well."

People kept walking as they talked, their voices carrying down the path behind them.

Sahay watched her uncle carefully, but he never motioned her to jump off the path and hide. He walked quickly—no worry about hitting feet against stones in the dark—and did not talk to her. But every time they came to a curve, Sahay's feet made themselves ready to run.

All that day Sahay and her uncle walked. When dusk settled onto the path, they ate what was left of the *arah* and *saweh*. "In the morning, we will leave the basket here," her uncle said. "On this long trip, we will be glad of fewer things to carry."

For a long time, Sahay wrapped her arms around the basket and rested her head against it, smelling the sweet straw smell. One more thing from home to leave behind. Finally, she was so tired that she curled on the ground with her head on a stone, her arms still around the basket.

▲ ▼ ▲

The next morning, the path led them into the mountains. They saw no other people that day—only a leopard running through a grove of trees. The next day, they did not stop to rest even though it was the Sabbath. They said only quick prayers, facing in the direction of Jerusalem. Then they went on walking, up steep slopes of mountains and down into flat valleys with rivers running through them. When they had to pick their way through streams or rivers, Sahay was glad the rains had not come this year.

"We must try to save the food in our bags," her uncle said over and over. "I don't know how long the trip will be." So Sahay tried to keep her fingers from unknotting the food bag, even when her stomach growled with hunger. Though she had been hungry before, she had never known the hunger that came from walking with so little food.

On the afternoon of the fourth day, they saw some fields where the barley was growing strong, almost ready for harvest. Looking at the fields, Sahay ached for the month of Magabit, the time of sowing when the priest would bless the seeds so the earth would give birth another season. She limped behind her uncle, crossing one stream and then another, and she knew this must be a place of good water. As they came to the top of a hill, she looked down to see a small village. Children were playing at the edge.

"Perhaps they have food in this village," Sahay

said. She thought of the many times that other Kemant had come to her family's house and had gone on their way with food. Why shouldn't she, now, go into this village and come away with food?

Her uncle frowned. "It's not good to go near an unknown village."

Sahay stopped. But how could these children, who reminded her so much of herself and her cousins, be dangerous? The very thought of food made her dizzy with longing. "We have had hardly anything to eat," she whispered. "I've seen you stumble many times, too, and I am afraid that soon one of us will be seized by the sickness that grabs you and spins you around and sits you down."

Her uncle looked at her thoughtfully. "Well," he said. "You are just a child. And one can never know where a good person lives. Perhaps they will have pity on you and give you food."

"Let me ask." Sahay looked at his face. The caution there made her stomach jump with fear. But she was so hungry. They must have something to eat. As Sahay walked down toward the children, her head felt light. She thought she could almost float away on the small wind that carried the smells of food up to her.

The children did not look up from whatever game they were playing until she was very close. *What did my uncle think might happen?* she asked herself nervously. They were only children, not like the men who had come crashing down on her house that day of the terrible running and shouting. Still, she began to walk more and more slowly, putting one foot carefully in front of the other. "May God give you health for my sake," she finally called to them. "I need help and a little food."

A little girl looked up and screamed. She jumped up and ran back toward the village.

"Buda," one of the boys cried out. "Go away, *buda.*"

"No. I'm not a *buda.*" Sahay took a step forward.

One of the other boys scooped up a stone. Before Sahay could think what to do, the stone flew through the air and hit her arm.

Then the others picked up stones. Sahay turned and began to run. The stones hit her shoulder, the back of her head. *"Buda,"* she could hear them shout as she scrambled up the hill. *"Buda, buda."*

Her uncle was suddenly there in front of her and she stumbled into his arms. "Sahay!" She felt his arms holding her and then his hands guiding her. "Quickly," he said. "Kneel by this stream." She felt cold water splashing against the back of her head. "I should not have let you go."

Sahay turned and cried against his shoulder. "But we will die unless we get more food," she whispered finally. "Why did they call me *buda?*"

Her uncle clicked his tongue ruefully. "They were probably Amhara. Our stories say that even though the Kemant have been in these mountains since the beginning of time, when the Amhara came—many, many generations ago—they became Ethiopia's rulers. As the saying goes, 'Amhara were made to be rulers, not to be ruled.' "

Sahay remembered the way her mother would carelessly point out a group of people in the *markato* and tell her that they were Amhara people from such and such a village. Sahay would stare at the Amhara people, but they looked just like Kemant people. And did she and her uncle not speak the Amhara's language?

"The Amhara say Kemant and Falasha are *budas*," her uncle continued. "The Kemant say the Falasha are *budas*. Whenever misfortune comes, everyone looks for someone to blame. And these days, there is great misfortune throughout the country."

Her uncle took her arm and guided her to a place a little way from the stream, where they could hide. Sahay's head pounded and she was not hungry any longer. She thought angrily that she would not eat the children's food, even if they had given her some. How dare they call her *buda*?

Late that night, she heard her uncle get up without a word and walk away, his bare feet making almost no sound in the darkness. Next morning, he gave her grain and chickpeas to fill up her bag. She did not ask where he had found them.

▲ ▲ ▼ ▲ ▼ ▲ ▼ ▲ ▼ ▲ ▼ ▲ ▼ ▲ ▼ ▲ ▼ ▲ ▼ ▲

The Beads

That night, after the meeting was over, Rahel lay awake thinking about the Exodus story, trying to imagine what the children of Israel felt like as they baked the unleavened bread for their journey, as they got ready to leave Egypt and everything they had ever known. Finally, she fell asleep. But a dark, flapping shape flew at her in her dreams, and she woke, crying out.

Grandmother whispered, "Has the fear caught you again?"

Rahel pulled her *gahbi* around her chin. "We've been told we belong in Jerusalem. But how can we leave this place for a faraway country? I have never been out past the warm places of my home."

"Come here, child." Grandmother bent and blew on the fire. Rahel heard it spurt to life, and then heard Grandmother pick up the spindle. "Long, long ago, the Emperor Tewodros was king of Ethiopia. His rule was a proud moment of Ethiopian history for us because our old stories say that his father and mother were both Beta-Israel, though no one knew it. During Emperor Tewodros's reign, visitors from far away came to travel all over Ethiopia—from north to south, from east to west. Everywhere they went, they made maps of the mountains and the lakes and the rivers and the waterfalls. When they had seen all the beauty of Ethiopia, they came back to the king."

Rahel rested her head against her grandmother's shoulder. Grandmother's voice was like the song of her flute, making Rahel feel calm and strong.

"The king was pleased. He ordered a great feast and gave the visitors gifts of gold and silver. Then the visitors returned to their ships on the Red Sea. But as they started to board their ships, the king's servant stopped them. One by one, he took off their shoes. One by one, he washed each shoe. 'Thus says the king,' the servant said. 'You have seen all of Ethiopia and you know that it is very beautiful. You may take the gold and silver, but I will not give you our greatest treasure—the earth.' "

Rahel reached up. Grandmother's face felt like soft cloth in the firelight. "How do we make pottery?" Grandmother asked.

"From the earth," Rahel whispered.

"Rahel." Grandmother's voice was gentle. "You have no choice about going on this journey. But if you take one of our pots with you, you can take a part of your home."

Grandmother shifted and put something into Rahel's hand. When Rahel closed her hand around it, she knew it was the amber beads her grandmother had always worn around her neck. They were warm like Grandmother's skin.

"These beads will help you take something even more important," Grandmother said. "They are a storyteller's beads, and I give them to you for your journey. During the days until you go, I will tell you our stories. Every time you touch a bead, you must remember its story." She guided Rahel's fingers to the first bead after the knot. "This one holds the story of the Emperor Tewodros and his visitors."

Rahel pushed the beads away. Her voice trembled. "But I want *you*. You have been the one to take care of me and show me things ever since my eyes could no longer see for themselves."

Grandmother's voice was soft. "The *aliyah* is starting, and I know you will be strong. Only God knows if you will ever reach Jerusalem. But as you remember each story, you'll hear my voice and I will be with you." She put the beads around Rahel's neck.

Rahel closed her eyes, smelling the wood smoke and the spices on her grandmother's hands. She could hear Grandmother's bones creak as she lay down. Rahel's fingers curled around the beads. Learning the stories—yes, that would be wonderful. But she was not going to give up on Grandmother's going to Jerusalem. She fell asleep chanting softly to herself. "If Grandmother is not going, I will not go, either. If Grandmother is staying, I will find a way to stay."

For three days, as they went about their work, Grandmother told stories—old stories and new stories—putting one story with each bead. "Now you say the story," she would say. "The stories will keep you strong."

Rahel said the stories back, loving the feel of the words in her mouth. Grandmother made her work hard to remember every word of the story of Hirute. "This story is an especially beloved one for our people," Grandmother said. "After all, Hirute was an ancestor of King Solomon, and you know how important the story of King Solomon is to Ethiopia. Remember: The Beta-Israel always welcome the stranger who accepts our religion the way the people of Israel accepted the stranger Hirute."

After most stories, Grandmother would pat Rahel's cheek and say, "You are a wonderful storyteller, just as I knew you would be." Sometimes, though, she scolded and said, "Where has your attention flown?" Rahel did not reply. She could hardly admit that she had been trying to think of something that would change Grandmother's mind about going.

On the fourth morning, Father said, "Come, Rahel. I need your help." Father drove the oxen down the path, while Rahel carried the hoe and ax, her hand on Father's shoulder. "Remember," Father said. "Do not say anything about Jerusalem to anybody. Many Ethiopians are leaving because of the hunger, and such a thing is not seen as unpatriotic, but to talk about belonging in another place . . ." He clicked his tongue.

"I remember," Rahel said calmly, but her face felt suddenly hot with fear. Was the *aliyah* here? Today? It was too soon. She hadn't yet thought of what to say to Grandmother.

After a while, Father stopped and greeted someone. When Rahel heard the man's return greeting, she knew it was an Amhara man who lived nearby and owned many fields. When the greetings were over, Father said, "Perhaps you would like to buy these things of mine."

"The cloth and pottery you have sold me have always been strong," the man said. "So I will buy your tools. But why are you going?"

Rahel tensed. What would Father say? Under her hand, she felt his shrug. "You see how it is," he said. "The rains do not come."

Rahel waited nervously, but the neighbor said only, "Go with God. I am sorry I will not be able to buy things from you any longer."

They had not gone far on their way home when Rahel heard footsteps on the path. *Dawit,* she thought. Yes, there was his voice, greeting Father, whispering that Mother was baking *kita*, unleavened bread for the journey.

"Go on and do what I told you, then," Father said. "Remember, if anyone questions you, tell them we are leaving because of the famine."

Dawit made an angry sound. "I'm tired of always hiding, hiding. Can't we ever speak openly for our faith?"

"Do not grab a lion by the tail." Father's voice was sharp, but Rahel heard the fear in it. "You know that other Ethiopians have always been afraid of the Beta-Israel and our religious beliefs. Fear fills them with hate." His voice dropped to an ominous whisper. "Dawit, beware of the danger when you stir the pot of fear and hate."

For a moment, there was silence. Rahel felt herself shivering. Then Father said to her, "Now you will help your grandmother take care of selling pottery at the *markato*."

First, Grandmother and Rahel took eucalyptus leaves and rubbed all the pots and pitchers and cups, making the clay shine. Then they stacked the pieces and started walking to the village.

"Is there clay in Jerusalem?" Rahel asked.

Grandmother's feet made a soft padding sound in the dust. "I do not know. I have never been to Jerusalem."

Please go now, Rahel thought. *I don't want to go*

without you. Could she hide somewhere? Could she run to the house of one of her aunts? If Father found her, his anger would burn her up. Rahel touched Grandmother's beads for courage. Suddenly, she felt as beautiful as Queen Yehudit.

As they neared the village, Rahel heard a scratching noise. It was a sound made by children riding branches from trees, pretending the branches were horses. She and Dawit used to play the same way. She could still see, in her mind, the line the branch made in the dirt as she ran.

Suddenly, a child's voice called out, "Falasha. My father says the Falasha have stopped the rains."

Rahel's hand tightened on the beads. She had always been able to make herself small, had gotten in to no one's way, and the children had left her alone. But now, it seemed, each day brought more and more troubles for the Beta-Israel.

"Falasha," the children shouted now. *"Buda."*

"People of Yehudit," called one boy. "Yehudit Bud'it."

"Come, Rahel." She felt Grandmother's hand on her arm. But she was stiff as a piece of wood. "Come." Grandmother gave her a push, and her legs stopped being wood and became legs again.

As they hurried on into the village, they could hear the children chanting. "Yehudit Bud'it. Yehudit Bud'it."

Rahel did not speak until the pots were spread on

the ground at the *markato* and she and Grandmother had settled behind them. Then she cried out, "How could they call Queen Yehudit, the beautiful, a *buda*?"

Grandmother clicked her tongue. "Perhaps it is nature to blame someone else when things go wrong. Their teachers teach them to hate Queen Yehudit. Their parents call us Falasha, strangers. Yet even though they call us names—or worse—no one wants to let us leave Ethiopia."

Rahel pulled her *shamma* up to cover her head. Maybe it would not be so terrible to go to Jerusalem and wear white and pray all day. "But the man who bought our oxen was kind."

"Some of our neighbors who are not Beta-Israel have been kind," Grandmother said. "In some people, it seems to be their nature to be kind."

A woman came up and began to bargain for one of the pots. Rahel let the words ripple over her as she thought about what Grandmother had said. Ten years ago, when Haile Selassie, the king of kings, was overthrown by the military committee, her people had hoped their lives would be better. But here they were, still with land that was like an old, bony cow. With schools closed down. With fear always hanging in the air.

Buda. The echoes of the children's voices stung. It was true what the priests and elders had always said. This place that felt like home could never truly be home.

▲ ▼ ▲ ▼ ▲ ▼ ▲ ▼ ▲ ▼ ▲ ▼ ▲ ▼ ▲ ▼ ▲

Out of Ethiopia

Sahay sat with her bag in her lap. Her uncle shook her shoulder. "The time has come. We should go." But when she tried to get up, she stumbled and fell. Her head pounded where the stones had hit her. After a moment, she felt cold water on her face. Her uncle's voice sounded far away. "May God have mercy on you. Lie here on the grass until I return. No one will see you if you are quiet."

Where are you going? She thought she said the words to him, but he didn't answer, so perhaps the words were caught somewhere inside her mouth.

Sahay felt the ground swirl under her. As the sun climbed higher, she saw herself as a child, building small houses of sticks and mud with her cousins, throwing stones at monkeys to keep them out of the fields. Her oldest cousin, Waldu, was pretending to be a horse. He showed Sahay how a horse would kick and kick, and on the third kick his foot hit a clay pot.

As the water spilled through the broken clay onto the ground, she heard her uncle say, "Waldu! If you do not behave, a hyena will get you."

Oh, the last time she had seen Waldu ... Sahay whimpered.

"Hush." It was Waldu's voice. They were hiding in the corn, and the footsteps were everywhere around them, running, running. But Waldu was dead. How could he be speaking to her here? "Hush," she heard again. So she held herself still until she heard her grandmother humming. This was how her grandmother had hummed, long ago, when she taught Sahay how to spin.

"How impatient and stubborn you are," her grandmother would cry when Sahay yanked at the cotton instead of smoothing it gently with her fingers. Yes, she was stubborn. It was stubbornness, not courage, that made her escape to the cave on the day of the terrible running. She dug her fingers into the dirt beside her, wanting to cry. But stubbornness had also kept her working hard in this year of her sadness, not letting her thoughts seize her. It kept her walking, now, day after day. Now the Red Terror was burning brighter, burning up her stubborn strength.

Sahay felt pinpricks on her arms. In the swirling, she thought her grandmother and mother were giving her another tattoo, dipping acacia thorns in the dark dye made from *nug* oil and soot, and then poking her skin with the thorns, as they had made the design on her forehead. "The tattoo will also keep away the evil eye that comes to beautiful girls," she heard her grandmother say.

How could her grandmother be speaking to her? She had seen her grandmother's body with her own eyes, right there, lying beside Waldu. She shook the swirling from her head. "Enough," she said to the spirit that must be bringing her these strange thoughts and voices. But the pricking did not stop. When she put her hand to the burning place, she pulled off the body of a black ant. No mother, no grandmother. Just ants.

Sahay used her father's walking stick to help drag herself down to the stream where the mud and water cooled her hurting arms. She did not know how long she lay by the water. After a time, she felt her uncle's arms lifting her. Then something warm was at her lips. Milk. Sahay and her cousins had stopped drinking milk when they were just little children. She drifted into sleep.

Late that night, Sahay woke to a sweet smell from better times. Her head seemed to have come back to her again. The smell was coming from a small fire where her uncle was roasting corn. When she moved, he came and bent over her, his face wrinkled with fear.

"The spirit that was giving me strange half dreams is gone," Sahay said.

"How great is our joy together! Eat this corn and you will feel stronger."

She did feel stronger after she ate the corn and drank more milk. She knew the taste of hunger well from each year before harvest when the food had almost run out, and from the long fasts that people said were like the bit in the mouth of a horse. Fasting was important, but it was a hard discipline. "Praise be that you have survived the bit of the fast," people would say to each other when it was finally time to eat again. Food never tasted sweeter than at harvest or after a fast. But Sahay had never tasted food as good as this food. "Where did you find milk?" she asked.

"Not all Amhara people are our enemies," her uncle answered. "A farmer sold me some food. When I told him my child was sick, he also gave me the milk."

After a few minutes, he continued. "Sahay, I have been thinking about our journey. The farmer helped me find something else we need. A guide. The day after tomorrow, when you are stronger, we will join a group of people who all left their homes as we did. The guide will help us find the way out of Ethiopia."

Out of Ethiopia. What were these strange words? What could the world possibly be like somewhere else? "How will we ever find our way back?" Sahay cried out.

"I do not think we will ever go back."

Anger leaped from Sahay's stomach to her throat to her face. She tried to push the words away, pretend he never said them. "We must go back! What about the house where my father and mother made everything? What about..." She forced herself to say it. "What about the graves?"

Her uncle's look darkened. "Do you think I've forgotten the graves? My own brother lies there—and my children. But all I can do for my brother now is take care of you as a daughter." He stood up, looming over her. "I will not let your life be snuffed out, too," he whispered fiercely.

Sahay began to shake. Yes, the strangers would snuff out everything if they could. But she could fight them by staying alive. "All right, then," she said. "Let's go." She wanted to scream the words, but screaming wouldn't help her to stay alive. Only stubbornness would.

"From now on," her uncle said, "we must hide not only from *shiftas* but also from the police and government troops. If they find us trying to leave the country, they will stop us and force us to go back."

Sahay held her head in her hands. Why would anyone care if such poor people left the country? What riches did she and her uncle have or what kind of work could they do that would make someone want them to stay?

"I know how strange my words must sound," her uncle continued. "The government does not care about Kemant farmers. But they find it insulting to think that anyone would want to leave. And as for me, the government does especially not want any men to leave the country because men are needed to fight the war against Eritrea."

Sahay had heard whispers of the government troops that came to drag men and boys from their homes to force them to be soldiers. But she had not wanted those stories to be true. And old men? Like her uncle? Oh, this could not be. Could it?

When they began to walk again, they left the path and picked their way over stones that bruised Sahay's feet. Sometimes she had to push her way through thick bushes with branches that scratched her legs. Her father's walking stick kept her from falling, and her anger kept her feet moving forward. She would stay alive, no matter what. Her feet began to bleed. "Only a little more," her uncle whispered. "Everybody is gathering in a place not far from here. Are you strong?"

She didn't want to answer. Somehow, the days of her life were being sewn together wrong. Everything was wrong. They would be traveling with strangers now, eating their food—whatever food there was—in front of strangers. No matter what kind of stubborn strength she had, some stranger's evil eye would probably find a way to try to snuff her out.

▲ ▼ ▲ ▼ ▲ ▼ ▲ ▼ ▲ ▼ ▲ ▼ ▲ ▼ ▲

Leaving

At supper the next night, Rahel's father said, "We have done all we can. We have water jugs, a little food, and a little bit of medicine. Tonight, when there is no moon, we will begin the trip."

Rahel dropped the piece of *injera* she had been holding. The words slapped against her ears. For all the days of getting ready, the *aliyah* had swooped down on her while she still didn't have a plan.

She heard Dawit scramble to his feet. "I wish I had a gun. I'm going to go cut a strong branch for when we meet dangers in the night."

"Sit down!" Father's voice was the roar of a wounded animal. "The most important thing now is to say farewell to your grandmother and sit quietly until the signal comes."

Say farewell? Never. Rahel groped for her bag and put it in her lap. Grandmother had helped her pack her flute, a small pot, a little food. Now she must find some way to help Grandmother pack. She was not going without her. Her father spoke more softly now. "*Emayay,* will you not think again about coming with us on our journey?"

"It is the nature of the old to want to stay with what they know." Grandmother's voice was calm and stubborn. "Also, I do not want to slow you down."

"So be it," Father said. "You have made your choice."

Rahel rubbed the cloth of the bag until her fingers found the rounded edge of the pot and then the tip of the flute. How could her father give in so easily? What could *she* do? She wanted to pull the flute from the bag and play something—notes of longing, notes of pain.

What if Grandmother were right and this was a trip only for the young and strong? Rahel wondered if she, herself, was strong enough to make it. She stroked one of the beads with her fingertip. All those strong people. Deborah and Rahel. Sara and Queen Yehudit and Hirute. Others, also. Yes, she could be strong, too. She could take her place in this exodus. But was it truly best for Grandmother to stay?

She tried to think about what it would be like to be Grandmother all alone in the house with her family gone. Rahel imagined herself as Grandmother, waking up the next morning, listening to the house. What would the house say? It would say *chrrrrr, chrrrr,* the sound of seeds rattling in a dry gourd. No, it couldn't be best to be alone.

Rahel put her bag down and made her way to kneel beside her grandmother. "We have all heard how there is no food in the north," she whispered. "What will you do when the food is gone here, too?"

"Come," Rahel's mother said. "You must not question your grandmother."

Sadness and fear rose in Rahel's throat. She knew better than to lift her face directly at her mother and father. But she had to do something.

The silence grew long. What could a blind girl do? Suddenly Rahel thought of Sampson—Sampson, the strongest man in all of Israel. After he broke his promise not to cut his hair, he became so weak that his enemies were able to capture him and make him blind. She imagined what it was like to be Sampson, standing in the middle of his enemies' taunts. She felt pillars against her back, the pillars Sampson had felt. What had Sampson done? He had reached for the pillars and pulled the roof down on top of everybody, including himself. Well, her parents were not her enemies, but she could find courage in the story. She would pull down pillars, too.

"Mother and Father," Rahel said. "Forgive me for speaking out." She paused for a moment. They must be staring at her. Mother must be opening her mouth to say, "Didn't I give you butter when you were a baby to make your voice soft and respectful? What are you doing?"

But before anyone said anything, Rahel rushed on. "All my life, I have heard the story of Queen Yehudit. So though I have been told that women must be quiet and patient, perhaps sometimes things become so terrible that even a girl must speak."

Rahel stopped. The quiet in the *tukul* drummed on her ears. She tried to make her voice firm. "It is Grandmother's nature to want to stay with what she knows, but she shouldn't stay here alone. If Grandmother will not go, I think I should stay with her. I am only a blind girl and will not be missed in Jerusalem."

She wanted to fold her arms over her chest, but she left them at her side. Looking obstinate would only make Father more angry. Far away, she heard a donkey's screeching bray. Was a new Moses out there somewhere, getting ready to rise up and lead?

Finally, Father spoke. "You have never given us worry until this night, Rahel." His voice was angry.

Rahel bowed her head. Suddenly, Grandmother said, "Do not be angry with the girl. It may be that only the strong-willed will survive these times."

Father began to speak again, but Grandmother's voice pushed in. "Don't forget. I am an old woman and it is in the nature of the old to be wise. So I hear my own words coming back to my ears. Rahel has only listened to the wise things I have told her."

Rahel reached for Grandmother's hand and drew it up to the beads. "Grandmother," she whispered.

"Haven't our elders always told us our true home is far from here? Haven't you always said the same thing to me? It's time for us all to be leaving now, like Moses did, even if we have to wander for forty years like the other children of Israel. We should not stay here alone to starve. We should take our place in the story."

There was a long moment of silence. Rahel held her breath, listening to the soft pop of an ember in the fire. Soon the embers would burn down to needlepoints of red in the gray ashes and then go out—for the last time?

Suddenly, she heard Grandmother shift to tighten her *gabbi* around her. "Oh Rahel," Grandmother said. "Perhaps you are right. Even an old woman and a girl would be missed if we did not to go Jerusalem."

A river of joy poured and bubbled from the top of Rahel's head to her feet. She had done it. She had changed Grandmother's mind. She pulled Grandmother's hand to her neck so that they were touching the warm beads together. She wanted to shout and dance. *Sampson, I pulled down the pillars. Deborah, I'm wise like you. Rahel, my father didn't win the way your father did. Sara and Abraham, I'm ready. I'm ready to follow you into the unknown.*

Suddenly, she heard someone running toward the *tukul.* Her hand tightened on Grandmother's. In a moment, the steps were at the door, and a neighbor's voice called out to her father.

Rahel heard rustling, whispers. Her breath leaped

in her and she began to tell herself the story of Queen Yehudit to slow it down. Her father was back before she got through it. "Dawit," he said. His voice was urgent. "Come and listen with all your ears to what I have to say."

Everyone's breathing stilled.

"The authorities have heard of the plan to leave," he continued. "They warned us if we try to leave, our men will be thrown in prison. You know what prison means for us. Torture. Perhaps death."

Rahel's throat burned. *What about Jerusalem?*

"A few of the young people can still slip away," Father whispered urgently. "A guide has been promised money. He waits, not too far from here. We do not want to lose the chance for some of our village to make *aliyah*."

The words began tumbling into Rahel's ears so fast that she could only catch hold of some of them. "Children...future...must go quickly..." Her mother's and grandmother's kisses were on both of her cheeks. Her father's hands were guiding her to the outside of the *tukul*. "Wait," she said. "Wait. Grandmother, you are my strength. I need you."

She heard her grandmother's voice in her ear. "Don't you see how strong you've become, Rahel? This time you will go first and make the path for me."

Rahel was standing in the cool night air. "Dawit," her father said, "you must take Rahel and go. We will come as quickly as we can."

Rahel felt arms around her again. She felt kisses on her face, her hands. "We will come." Mother's voice. "We will bring Grandmother with us."

"Wait, wait," Rahel said again. But there was no time to wait.

"Hear, Israel, the commandments of God." It was Father's voice in the words of the Sabbath prayer. "Adonay is one; his name is his alone."

And then Grandmother's voice. "You have your home with you. *Ayezosh*, be strong."

Then Rahel was walking with her hand on Dawit's shoulder. It was all too fast, too fast. The night, as always, was whispering. *Danger. Danger.* She tried not to think of hyenas that might be slinking through the rocks up ahead with their strange coughing cries and bitter eyes. "Do we have to leave at night?" she whispered, her hand tight on Dawit's shoulder.

"It's a good night to travel." Dawit's voice was excited and strong. "The stars are like drops of water that have caught the light, but there is no moon."

The stars. Abraham and Sara must have looked at those stars as they walked, thinking of their future children. In the distance, Rahel could hear the clopping of a mule or a horse on the path. "The place where we meet the guide is not too far from here," Dawit whispered. "But be ready to go off the path."

After a few minutes, Rahel could tell from the sounds that a few other people had joined them. "The trip will be hard," one of Dawit's friends whispered.

"But are we not the children of Abraham, Isahac, Yakob, and Solomon?"

"If we reach the Sudan," another of the young men said, "we will be taken to Jerusalem."

Rahel held tightly to Dawit's shoulder. "Do you think it was God or an angel who started the whisper in the *markato*?" she asked him.

"I don't think so." He hesitated and then said, "I think Beta-Israel who have reached Jerusalem are sending the word back."

"But even if we get to the Sudan, how will we find the other Beta-Israel? How will we even know who they are?"

She could feel impatience or anticipation trembling through Dawit. "I don't know. Here our people have been linked by family and years of living together. I don't know how it will be there. The important thing is that we're getting out of here."

Rahel touched the beads. She would have to hold on to the thought that she was one of the children of Israel, following Moses—or maybe Queen Yehudit riding off to Axum. The start of the road must have been scary for even those people. But no matter what happened to her on the road, she had won a victory tonight. Her blood and bones felt strong with joy as she thought of Grandmother coming after, following the path she and Dawit were making.

▲ ▼ ▲ ▼ ▲ ▼ ▲ ▼ ▲ ▼ ▲ ▼ ▲ ▼ ▲

Over the Mountains

Sahay stumbled and picked her way through the dark for a long time. Finally, her uncle stopped and whistled, a low, strange sound. She listened but heard only a call of a far-off night bird. Her uncle whistled again. This time, out of the darkness came a whistle.

Sahay clutched her uncle's *gahbi*. Except for the children who threw stones, she had not seen any other people for days. "*Ayezosh*," her uncle whispered. "It is just as the man told me it would be."

The ground opened its mouth ahead of them, and they had to find their way down into that mouth. When they reached a flat place, someone came out of the darkness so suddenly that Sahay thought it was a spirit until she heard his voice. After her uncle and the man spoke in harsh whispers for a few minutes, the three of them crept along the bottom of the ravine. Then Sahay's uncle helped her find a place on the ground, where she was able to lean against a rock. She knew there were other people around her because she could hear the breathing, but she could see nobody.

Sahay closed her eyes and slept, waking when she heard the sound of low voices. "More people," her uncle whispered. "Return to your sleep." When she woke again, the early-morning birds were calling. She looked around.

The group was twenty or thirty in all—some men, some women, teenagers, and children. A young woman near her carried a baby in an *ankelba* on her back. An old woman, probably a grandmother, jiggled a toddler on her hip. A man with a grave, patient face bent down to talk to a boy who was whimpering. A young woman, probably his wife, held on to the man's arm, and a little girl clung to the woman's dress. There was even a girl who had perhaps been born in the same year of Sahay's own birth. Sahay stared at the amber beads that glowed soft yellow around the girl's neck.

As the sun's warmth made its way down into the ravine, people began to move around and eat. Sahay still had a little corn, and, as she ate, she watched the girl with the beads untie her bag. The girl's fingers loosened the knot, but she stared straight ahead, not looking at her work. The young man who sat beside her took her hand and guided it to the water jug.

Sahay's uncle looked up and saw the girl she was watching. "Perhaps she was married to him to keep her safe," he whispered. "Sometimes parents find husbands for young girls to protect them from strange men on the road."

This girl, Sahay thought, was clearly blind. Surely, her parents had worried and wept as they sent her on to the road. With the corner of her *gahbi*, Sahay wiped at the tears that rimmed her eyes. Her own parents would have worried, too.

After a time, the guide stood up. He had a loud face, with a scar that started on his forehead and ended at his thin lips. He carried a gun over his shoulder. "We will walk only at night," he said. "If you or your children fall behind, we will not wait."

The mother put a protective hand back to touch her baby. Sahay looked at the blind girl. Her face made no sign that she had heard the guide.

The woman who sat beside the young man nudged him and made a gesture with her chin at the girl. "My sister can keep up," the young man told the woman, loud enough for everyone to hear. *So she is his sister and not his wife,* Sahay thought.

"No one must make noise in the daytime or in the night," the guide continued. "If the children cry, cover their mouths. Noise can bring *shiftas* or government troops."

Sahay thought the guide himself looked like a *shifta*. She had seen her uncle and other people give him money.

No one said anything. Finally, the guide spoke again. "You are the only people I will take. A small group can move quickly and stay away from the eyes of those who must not see." He stopped and looked around at each person. "But you must all keep up," he warned again.

The young man who was with the blind girl spoke. "Will we stop on the Sabbath?"

Sahay looked at him in surprise. He knew about the Sabbath. Was he Kemant, then?

"No," the guide said. "We will not stop."

Sahay heard others murmuring. Close to her ear, her uncle whispered, "We cannot stop for any reason." But the young man said, "We should stop on the Sabbath."

"I have guided many Falasha groups from here to the Sudan border." The guide's voice was angry. "Not one has stopped on the Sabbath. Do you think you are the only Falasha to make this journey?"

Falasha. Sahay sucked in her breath. So many terrible things had happened, and here was one more. They would be traveling with Falasha. She looked at her uncle, but he did not say anything. Well, she would keep far from them and not let herself become polluted. Already she had put herself in danger by looking at them for so long.

All that day, Sahay tried to rest, knowing she would be walking at night. But whenever she closed her eyes, fear churned her stomach. "*Ayezosh,*" she whispered to herself, in the same tone her mother would have used.

When the light began to fade from the sky, the guide whistled and people climbed, one by one, up out of the ravine. Three teenagers struck out quickly, making their way to the front. People with children tried to hurry them along, whispering "hush" as they went. Sahay saw the man with the patient face pick up his son to carry him on his back.

Branches and thorns tore at Sahay's clothes and skin, but she was glad to be doing something and not sitting. How could the blind girl walk? Sahay told herself not to look. But then she looked anyway. The girl was holding the shoulder of her brother. She did not cry out when a branch slapped her across the neck.

Soon, the way grew steep, and Sahay had to lean on her father's walking stick. Thirst came over her, thick as smoke in her throat, but when the guide led the group to a streambed, it was dry. Some of the people had cans they drank from, but Sahay and her uncle had no can.

Up and down they went over rough and stony ground. Sahay again wondered how the blind Falasha girl could find her way, but she did not want to look at her again. Had she ever seen a Falasha up close before? Suddenly, she remembered the time she and Waldu had hidden behind a tree, watching a blacksmith softening iron over a fire. *Whoosh. Whoosh.* Another Falasha used a goatskin bellows to blow the fire red-hot. Sparks flew up in a popping cloud. The strange smell of hot iron filled the air. Then the smith lifted the iron out of the fire and swung a black hammer, smashing it down on the glowing iron. That's when Waldu grabbed her hand and they had run away.

Remembering the strange smell, Sahay hugged herself, trembling. Perhaps this girl and her brother knew some kind of witchcraft to help them find their way. Perhaps if Sahay looked around, she would see two hyenas running through the dark.

A choking feeling grabbed Sahay's throat. She felt she could not breathe for the thirst. But she kept going, kept breathing. The guide led the way down over stones to another streambed, but this one, too, was dry.

Soon Sahay began to cough from the dust, but she covered her mouth to stop the noise. Her head began to swirl. She closed her eyes, swaying. The strength in her stomach was gone. She wasn't even sure where her uncle was. People began to push past. "No one must fall behind," a woman said, as she walked past.

Then Sahay felt someone press a water can into her hands. She lifted it to her lips and let the water trickle into her mouth, down her dry throat. "May God reward you," she whispered. As she opened her eyes, she saw with horror that it was the young man with the blind sister. She had drunk Falasha water.

Sahay spit on the ground. Suddenly, a fierce noise tore the night air. "Get down," the guide shouted. Sahay dropped her walking stick and fell down beside it. The sound cracked a second time. Someone was shooting a gun.

Sahay waited for death to come, but the guns did not shoot again. Instead, the guide said in a low voice, "Up. We must keep going."

Sahay heard her uncle whisper, "Sahay. Where are you?" She didn't dare call out, but she saw his white *gahbi* as he came toward her. He helped her up, and they stumbled on.

All that night they traveled. Night blurred into the next night, and still they kept going—for nine more nights. In the daytime, they curled up among the rocks, or in the dirt, to sleep. They did not dare build a fire for cooking, but, as people walked, they would grab a few handfuls of dried meat and grain from the bags they carried, or berries from the bushes they passed.

Many other times they heard distant gunfire. They climbed rocky ridges and left the blood of their feet on the stones there. Sahay watched as people threw away sandals, water cans—everything they could to make their loads lighter. She, herself, had nothing left to throw away.

Some days they traveled one behind the other on narrow paths, pressing bodies to the cliffs. Sahay knew she would fall for miles if she stepped in the wrong place. One time when she stopped, clinging to the cliff in terror, the smell of flowers drifted up from far below.

▲ ▲ ▼ ▲ ▼ ▲ ▼ ▲ ▼ ▲ ▼ ▲ ▼ ▲ ▼ ▲ ▼ ▲

Shiftas

Rahel's hand felt numb on Dawit's shoulder, her stomach tight with hunger. At first, she and Dawit and the others from their village had eaten together, sharing the unleavened travel bread they all had brought. Now, everyone was down to grain and dried peas. They ate bits of these when they must. She tried not to think of what would happen when the food was gone.

"What was Gondar like when you got to visit there?" Rahel whispered to Dawit to keep her mind off her stomach and one aching foot. She hoped the guide was far up at the front of the line and couldn't hear.

He panted a moment before starting to tell her, in a low voice, about the old capital and the stone castles built by the Ethiopian kings so long ago.

"Was the Emperor Tewodros one of them?"

"No, that was later. His capital was on the cliff of

Magdala. Listen, though." He continued. "In one of the castles in Gondar, the king and queen had separate dining rooms, tables, even shelves to put their crowns on. I heard one of the tour guides say the castles were built by Beta-Israel, but I do not know if that is true."

Rahel thought about that. It might be true. After all, her people had the secrets of working iron, why not stone? They had suffered much for their secrets. "And Addis Ababa?" she asked.

"The mountains were not so rugged as up here in the north. Cars ran everywhere like spiders on the roads." She felt him hesitate. "*Shhh*. I think the guide has stopped, Rahel. Wait here and let me go up the line and find out what's happening."

While she waited, Rahel rubbed at her foot until she found the thorn that was making it ache. She wondered where they were. Every night she would whisper to Dawit, "What does it look like here?" He would say, "Another deep gorge. We'll be going down into it and out the other side." Or "We have a sharp ridge to climb." Sometimes he said, "It's too dark to tell." She wondered, then, if he was just trying not to say frightening things.

She heard the light step of Dawit's feet. "This climb is one of the worst," he whispered. "People are throwing away anything they can to make the walk lighter. I saw an *ankelba* one woman had thrown away."

Rahel sucked in her breath. The only reason to

throw away an *ankelba* would be if the baby was no longer there to be carried in it.

"Rahel," Dawit said. "You need to throw away the pot you've been carrying. Maybe the flute, too."

She felt his fingers tugging at the bag. She curled her fingers tightly around it. "It's the earth," she wailed softly. "I cannot leave it."

"Rahel." She felt him move away. In a few minutes, he pressed something into her hand. "I scooped up some dirt for you in this little bag," he whispered.

She kissed the pot, then let him take it, holding tightly to the flute. She longed to put the flute to her lips, but of course she couldn't make that kind of noise here. For a moment, she rocked back and forth, clutching her shoulders with her hands. *Grandmother. Grandmother. Pack a smaller pot and bring it for me, Grandmother. Now only the stories are left.*

She felt Dawit's arm around her. "I hid it carefully between two rocks," Dawit whispered. "Perhaps someday someone will find it and see how lovingly you and Grandmother made it."

"I know you will be strong," Rahel thought she heard Grandmother say again. "As you remember each story, you'll hear my voice and I will be with you."

The next night, the climbing stopped and they began to descend. After a while, Rahel whispered, "How much longer must we go down? These paths down the cliffs, where you tell me, 'Hug the rock, hug the rock,' make my stomach swoop into my mouth.''

"We have gone over great crumpled mountains and down into ravines and back up,'' Dawit said. "But now we are close to the edge of Ethiopia. Our guide says that to reach the Sudan, we must walk down these last mountains to the flat grasslands.''

Rahel thought about Mother and Father and Grandmother. Had they already started their journey? What would Grandmother think of these cliffs where the path dropped into nothingness on one side? "We're trying to make a path for you, Grandmother,'' she whispered.

That night, the air seemed as quiet as if the long-gone rains might come again to water the steep passes. They had walked so long, Rahel was thinking only of sleep. When she heard the low whistle, she paid no attention. It was some mountain bird. But Dawit stopped.

The guide's voice hissed through the dark. "*Shiftas.* Scatter and hide. Behind rocks—or try that ravine.''

"Hurry.'' Dawit gave her a little push. "This way. You'll have to use both hands to fight the thick bushes.''

Rahel let go of Dawit's shoulder and began to shove at the branches. They scratched her, and she felt a thorn tear her dress. She could hear other people scrambling over the rocks, through the bushes. Sudden shouts filled her ears. The air was alive with noise. Rahel reached out, but Dawit was nowhere.

She could tell by the way the air had changed that she must be at the mouth of the ravine. She forced her way in and pressed up against the side.

"Quiet," someone hissed, so she stopped moving. Dirt fell into her hair and down the neck of her dress. A child whimpered and someone covered his mouth. For a moment, Rahel heard only panting. Then voices. Footsteps.

Men called to each other and beat at the bushes above the ravine with heavy sticks. More dirt dropped onto Rahel's neck. Her breath was so loud it would surely bring the *shiftas* down into the ravine. She covered her mouth to stop the sound.

Beside her, someone whimpered. Rahel reached out and felt a smooth arm. The person grabbed Rahel's fingers. Just outside the ravine, a sharp wail rose and was choked off. Rahel gasped. Even when the noises moved away a little, she did not dare move. Nobody moved. The smells of dirt and leaves filled her head. She eased her free hand up to her waist and felt for the flute, the little bag of earth. Good. The bushes had not been able to tear them away.

She wanted to say her prayers, but who knew which way to turn to face Jerusalem, here in this ravine? A bit of a prayer came to her anyway. "Deliver me and put me with Israel, Thy people, Israel." Her free hand went automatically to the beads. Which one was she touching? Of course. This one Grandmother had made her say over and over so many times. She heard Grandmother's voice begin the story:

After her two sons died, Nahomey set out from the place where she was living to return home to the land of Israel. Her two daughters-in-law from that land, Orpah and Hirute, went with her on the path. But Nahomey said to her two daughters-in-law, "Do I have more sons for you to marry? Go. Return, each of you, to your mother's house. May the Lord deal kindly with you, as you have dealt with me and my sons, who are now dead. The Lord grant that you may find a home, each of you here in your own land!" Then she kissed them, and they lifted up their voices and wept.

And they said, "No, we will return with you to your people."

But Nahomey said, "Turn back, my daughters; why will you go with me? Turn back, my daughters; go your way."

Orpah kissed her mother-in-law and turned back, but Hirute clung to her. And Nahomey said, "See, your sister-in-law has gone back to her people and to her gods; return after your sister-in-law."

But Hirute said, "Entreat me not to leave you or to return from following after you; for where you go I will go, and where you lodge I will lodge; your people shall be my people, and your God my God; where you die I

*will die, and there will I be buried. May the Lord do so
to me and more also if even death parts me from you."*

*And when Nahomey saw that Hirute was deter-
mined to go with her, she said no more.*

Near the ravine, a gun coughed sharply, saying
death, death. Where was Dawit? Rahel held tightly to
the beads, trying not to cry out. Could she live if
death leaped up and parted Dawit from her? No,
no—surely not. As Hirute knew, all people need
someone who will go with them and not leave them
all alone on the path. *Hirute,* Rahel whispered silently
in her stomach. *You left your home and made a safe
journey to Israel. Was it ever so terrible as this?*

The Cave

Once before, Sahay had hidden to save her life. Now the gunshot blasts made her want to scream. Where was her uncle? What if this time he was the one lying dead when she crawled out of the cave? She clung to the hand of the person beside her, trying to push the memories away. But she couldn't. She put her other hand to her mouth, but the sounds leaked out anyway, and she could feel tears running down onto her fingers.

"Sh-sh," she heard the person whisper. "The *shiftas* may come back."

But Sahay couldn't stop.

"Tell me," the whisper came then. "Tell me what's wrong."

"I hid." The words were like dirt in her mouth. "I hid in the dark of a cave for a whole day. Even when my back got cold and wet against the rock of the cave, I didn't move. That evening, when everything grew quiet, I came out to find my family. But what did I find? They were dead, all of them." She forced out the words. "My grandmother fell beside one cousin, with her arms around my youngest cousin. The strangers killed them all—my strong father, my strong mother, playful Waldu. Everyone but my uncle who was away at the *markato*."

All year, Sahay had felt as if this story would sting her mouth if she ever tried to tell it. Now, her breath hurt the back of her throat. But she had told the story. All of it. Well, all except the most horrible part. The part she didn't even dare think about.

Sahay felt the other person's hand smoothing her fingers as she cried. *"Ayezosh, ayezosh."* Finally, when the tears had left her feeling dry as sand, she slept.

In the morning, Sahay woke to dim green light. She looked at the hand that still curled around her own hand. *No!* It belonged to the Falasha girl. She pulled her hand away quickly. Her stomach clenched, and she thought she might throw up. Then, to her shame, she felt a small stirring of gladness to know that someone else from the group was still alive. Anyway, she had held the girl's hand all night. The Falasha girl had not turned into anything horrible. Sahay would surely have felt it if she had.

Without opening her eyes, the girl whispered, "Will you help me find my brother?"

Sahay was afraid to say yes. But she thought of the Amhara farmer who gave her milk. Perhaps if he could help her, she could help even a Falasha this one time. "Do you think the *shiftas* are gone?" Sahay whispered. "What if they are hiding in the forest above us, waiting for us to wake up?"

"I can't hear them anymore," the girl replied.

Sahay had always wondered, a little, if Falashas spoke some mysterious, hidden language. But here the girl was, speaking Amharic just as she did. Sahay listened. Perhaps the guide or someone would give a signal. She heard only soft breathing. "I wonder where my uncle is," she said finally.

"Is he your uncle? My brother said there was a girl who was traveling with her father."

"No." Sahay swallowed, feeling pain run up her throat.

"Yes, I understand it all now," the girl said quickly. After a while, she added, "I think I have felt a little of the grief you have felt—when we had to leave our father and mother and grandmother."

For a while, Sahay did not say anything more. Then she said, "We can't sit here until we grow into the earth like plants." So she and the girl pushed their way up through the bushes and out of the ravine.

One at a time, others crawled out from their hiding places. When Sahay saw her uncle's face, with dried blood where the thorns had scratched it, she cried out and held on to him tightly. The girl's brother also appeared. But the guide did not come to say what to do.

Finally, some of the men climbed up above the ravine to see what they could find. After a long time, they came back. Sahay saw that her uncle was carrying the guide's water can. "Killed. In the gunfire," he said. Some people of the group were also dead. The men had buried them as well as they could among the rocks and hard earth.

Sahay looked around. The three young teenagers who had set off so strongly at the front of the journey—gone. There were perhaps fifteen people left, standing close to one another. Sahay clung to her uncle as if he could save her from everything that was happening to them. "What can we do now?" someone asked.

"We will never survive," said a woman bitterly. Her child began to cry.

But the father with the patient face said, "The guide has brought us through the hardest part. If we can make it down this mountain, we will reach the flatland." When people shook their heads in disbelief, he insisted, "I have been this way once before, and I came back to bring my family out."

"There are lions in the flatland," someone said.

"Beware," someone else whispered. "Malaria walks in the flatland at midnight and noon. She looks like a tall, thin woman with uncombed hair."

But no one knew what to do if they did not keep walking. Sahay knew no one wanted to sit and wait for the *shiftas* to come back. So the group went on, following the man who had said he knew the way, as he picked out a path down the steep mountain. As she walked, Sahay thought about the people who had died. What about the rites of lamentation she and her uncle had given to her mother and father and grandmother, her aunt and cousins? Had her uncle been able to bury the guide and the other people with their faces to the east, as one should? And what about the *tazkar,* the second funeral that lets a person be content beyond the grave? These people would have no second funeral.

Now they traveled by day. During that day and all the next, the air became hotter and hotter. The group had to stop often to drink mouthfuls of water from the cans they carried. Sahay thought she had been hot before, but she had never felt the kind of hot dry wind that rushed to greet them as they walked down the last mountain.

That evening they reached the desert grasslands. Sahay could see no path, only tall yellow grass that made a dry brushing sound as she walked through it. Behind her were the mountains; ahead, only yellow grass. But the group stayed together and shared the little water they had. When a child was bitten by a snake, people took turns carrying him until he could walk again. For three days, they traveled by day and night, stopping only when they could go no farther. At night they heard the roars of lions out in the grass and smelled their fetid scent.

The hot ground made blisters swell on everyone's feet. When the water ran out, the group walked for two days and nights without any. Now everyone was out of food. But it was thirst that was so terrible. When finally Sahay was sure they would all die in the desert wasteland, a rainstorm opened the gates of the sky. Sahay felt the drops on her hot and dusty head. She and her uncle stood with their heads back and mouths open, letting the water run in. When the rain stopped, everyone scrambled to scoop water into their cans from small pools that had formed in the holes that dotted the rocks.

That night the Falasha girl took a wooden flute from her pack and began to play. When Sahay heard the sadness of the song that drifted over the grasslands, she thought of her mother and father. Tears would have come to her eyes except that her tears had dried up from the heat.

"Listen," a mother said to her child. The child stopped whimpering for a moment as the flute's sound floated over everyone.

"My brother told me to throw it out in the mountains," the girl said to the person beside her. "But it is light. I haven't played it before because we had to be quiet. Here, in this ruined place, I think there is no one—only lions and snakes—to hear us."

Sahay thought the Falasha girl was surely right. But she was not. The next day, they met another group of ragged people stumbling in the same direction they were going. Soon, among the hills they had come to, they met more people, until there were about a hundred, limping in ragged groups away from Ethiopia.

Sahay's uncle spoke with some of the new people and told her it was only a day or two to reach the Sudan border. "There is a camp," he said. "We will find food in the camp—and water."

Sahay thought of the dreams she'd had, only weeks before, of living beside a stream and never carrying water again. She would have laughed, but her laughter had dried up, too, and only her stubbornness kept her walking at all.

The next afternoon, as she stumbled along, she heard hoofbeats. Everyone looked around, but the heat had dried up even the ability to be afraid. Anyway, there was no place to hide this time, no bushes, nothing but grass. All they could do was stand as if they were asleep, dried up and thirsty, as the soldiers on horseback rode up over a small rise.

▲▼▲▼▲▼▲▼▲▼▲▼▲

The Desert

Nobody moved, as the horses galloped up. There was no place to run. The men on the horses had guns, and they...? They, Sahay thought, were only a ragged patch on the wide yellow cloth of the desert. She hid her face in the corner of her uncle's *gahbi*.

The talk beat at her ears, as she stood feeling the hot ground against her bare feet. "Money," the soldiers said. "Money." But no one in the group had any money left. "You shall not pass," the leader said. "Return to your villages. There is nothing for you here."

But there is nothing for us there. No one spoke the words, but Sahay could hear them in the air.

People began to turn, defeated. What could anyone do? Suddenly, one of the old women of the group, a *baaltet,* called up to the men on the horses. "Why do you try to stop us from leaving? One palmful of people, mostly women and children. Of what use are we to you?"

Sahay looked around, astonished at her courage. The leader stared down from his horse at the ragged group. If he told his horse to move, the old woman would be trampled.

Others murmured aloud then. "What do you want with us? Why do you stop helpless people?"

The leader raised his hand. "The women and children may go," he said. "But our country needs every man. Every man can be of use in fighting our war against the rebellious north."

Sahay cried out and held on to her uncle's *gahbi*. "No," she said. "No, you are all I have left."

"Go on," the leader shouted, "before I change my mind. Your men must return to the villages."

"I will not go on," Sahay whispered. "I will return with you." *Return to where?* she thought. *We have no home.*

But her uncle took her face and kissed her on both cheeks in the way of both greeting and parting. "I will soon be old," he said. "What does my life matter? Besides, I may have other chances to escape."

Stubbornness hardened Sahay's stomach. "No," she said. "I will not be separated from you."

Her uncle said the words Sahay had heard him say at the beginning of the journey. "Sahay. You are the only young one left of our family. If you do not carry our family's future with you into this new place, our family will disappear."

She wanted to again say *no* to her uncle. *Don't make me go.* But she was too tired and weak to say anything at all.

Sahay thought she could not bear to leave him. But she had borne so many things already that she took a step even as her mind was saying *no, no.* Suddenly, she held out her father's walking stick. She kissed her uncle's hand and put the walking stick in it. "You've lost yours," she whispered. "You'll need one for climbing the mountains again."

He kissed her on both cheeks once more and said, "Remember, Sahay. You are the flame of our family that will not be snuffed out." As she turned to watch him go, she saw the man with the patient face, who had escaped before. His young wife was talking to him in a soft, agitated voice, her hands fluttering like wounded birds. He put their son in her arms and then stood, for a moment, with his arms around them all. He had come back for his family, and now he would not be able to go with them into the Sudan. Through the weariness and the blinding heat, Sahay felt bitter anger rise up, burning her throat.

Then, to the side, she saw the blind Falasha girl. Her brother stood holding her hand. "You," one of the men on the horses shouted at him. "Start moving. Perhaps the girl will die soon in the desert, and you can be rid of her before you reach the mountains."

But she had walked this whole way with her hand on her brother's shoulder! Suddenly, Sahay could not stand one more bit of cruelty. What did she care if the girl put the evil eye on her? "Come," she said to the brother. "Put her hand on my shoulder. She can walk with me."

"May God reward you," he said. He took the girl aside, and they whispered together for a minute. Sahay looked to see what her uncle would think of this strange gesture of hers, but he was already walking slowly back toward the mountains, with the soldiers close behind. One of the soldiers reached down and shoved a man who was falling behind. Her uncle's *gahbi* was ripped, and his shoulders looked thin and sad. *Turn around,* she wanted to call to him. *Turn around and let me look at your face one more time.* But he just kept walking.

"Come," the *baaltet* said to a woman who was weeping in the sand. "We will go to the Sudan." Sahay's legs felt numb. She thought she couldn't take a step. Then the blind girl whispered, "Perhaps the soldiers will get tired of guarding a ragged pack of people. Perhaps the men will soon be able to turn around and find us."

So Sahay took one step and then another. The high-pitched sound of the desert insects was like screaming coming from inside her head and out her ears. The blind girl's hand was light on Sahay's shoulder, but she could feel, from the way it shook, that the other girl was trembling.

They walked all day. Sometimes they were silent, and sometimes a woman would cry out and others would join her until the mourning sound enclosed them like a blanket. The grasses cut their legs. In the late afternoon, they reached a place of hot, sharp stones and thorny acacia trees. The heat became even more cruel, and they huddled under the gray, brittle acacia trees for shade until the sun dropped low in the sky so they could go on. Huge rocks rose out of the desert. Not a spot of green was anywhere in sight. Sahay longed for the cool highland breezes, the mountains of her home.

All that day, the blind girl did not say a word, and Sahay did not speak to her. But as deep night came and they sat close to each other for warmth, Sahay said to the girl, "What is your name?"

"Rahel." The girl said nothing more and turned away.

"My name is Sahay." They fell asleep resting against each other's back.

The group began to walk before light, before the heat of the day seized them and made them weak again. Soon after the sun came up, they heard the sound of hoofbeats for a second time. A few women ran to crouch behind rocks. Most were too weak to move.

As the men rode up, though, Sahay saw they were not dressed as the government troops had been. "Northern rebels," one of the women whispered. The women with children pulled them close, and everyone stood waiting. Sahay could feel the girl's hand resting on her shoulder, but Rahel did not ask what was happening.

The soldiers came so close that Sahay could smell the sweat on the horses. "Don't worry," one of them called. "In about three hours, you will be at the Atbara River. On the other side is the Sudan." As they rode off, the horses' feet kicked up puffs of dust.

Without a word, the women and children began to walk again, stumbling through the hot, bleached grass. The Atbara River? How would they cross? Sahay thought of how the water around her home became angry in the month of Nahase, when the streams were swollen with rain. Those who dared to wade into such water often drowned. "Have we come so far to be stopped by a river?" she asked Rahel.

"No." Rahel's voice was steady. "Let me tell you the story of Moses and the Red Sea. It will keep our courage strong."

Rahel's voice was scratchy with dryness, but she told the story wonderfully; and, for a few minutes, Sahay forgot the broken thorn trees and the burning yellow of the land that stung her eyes. When Rahel told of Moses holding up his rod and watching the waters part, though, Sahay clicked her tongue softly.

Heat had made this girl crazy. But when they could finally see the Atbara River, Sahay gave a weak laugh.

"Why do you laugh?" Rahel asked. "Tell me what you see."

"How great is our joy together. We don't need Moses. The riverbed is as dry as everything else."

When they had climbed the banks on the other side of the dry riverbed, the women sank down onto the hot sand and stared at one another.

Finally, the old woman who had a child with her gave a small trill of joy. "We have reached the Sudan," she said, with a touch of defiance. "When my daughter was dying, up in the highlands of home, I promised her I would bring her child safely here. I have kept my promise."

Yes, Sahay thought. She, too, had followed her uncle's dream to reach a new country. *But what now?*

"Horses," Rahel whispered.

Sahay listened. Rahel was right. More soldiers rode up—Sudanese soldiers, this time. "Only a few," Sahay told Rahel, squinting up at the horses. "Four or five."

"My grandmother told me that one stone is enough against fifty clay pots," Rahel said. "How long ago it was that I heard her say that."

"Go back," the leader of the soldiers yelled in accented Amharic. "Things in Ethiopia are improving. You cannot stay here."

No one moved. Sahay felt as if they had all turned to clay. "I wonder whether the soldiers would want to pick up the pieces of fifty clay pots," she murmured to Rahel. Anyone who threw her out of the Sudan, she knew, would have to pick her up to do it. She would not walk one step back.

"Please," the strong old woman said. "You cannot send us back."

"Go back," they shouted.

Still, no one moved. The soldiers argued with one another in words Sahay didn't understand, while the women squatted with their *shammas* over their heads and waited. Finally, Sahay saw the leader wave his arms at his men, and, without a word, the soldiers rode off.

"Come," the *baaltet* said. A sigh rippled through the group, and they straggled on.

About noon the next day, they came upon some Sudanese people who had kind faces. A woman in the group who knew Arabic spoke to the people for some minutes. "They will show us the way to the Red Cross camp," she finally said. *Red Cross.* The words sounded strange in Sahay's mouth. "Umm Rekuba," she heard the Sudanese people say. Others repeated the name. "Umm Rekuba. Umm Rekuba."

The woman who knew Arabic translated. "The name of the camp means Mother of Shelter."

The women were so tired they could only shuffle their feet, but it was so near the end of the journey that no one wanted to stop. So they walked all that night. Near morning, Sahay heard the engine of a truck and moved, with Rahel, to the side of the rough track. "Umm Rekuba," the people in the truck shouted, as it rumbled by, throwing dust over everyone.

"We are almost there, I think," Sahay said to Rahel. *Almost there. Almost there.* She hardly dared to believe the trip would soon be over.

▲ ▼ ▲ ▼ ▲ ▼ ▲ ▼ ▲ ▼ ▲ ▼ ▲ ▼ ▲ ▼

PART 4

The Camp

▲ ▼ ▲ ▼ ▲ ▼ ▲ ▼ ▲ ▼ ▲ ▼ ▲ ▼ ▲ ▼ ▲

THIRTEEN

Umm Rekuba

Rahel put her *shamma* over her nose. "It doesn't smell like a mother of shelter," she said.

"No," Sahay said. "It doesn't.

Rahel's feet ached. She listened to the sun sizzling the grass around her and felt faint. There were times in the past few days when she had imagined Sahay and herself as two insects crawling across the desert under an angry sun. She'd had to concentrate on the other girl's shoulder under her hand to remember she was not an insect but a child of Abraham. Now they were almost there. "What do you see?" she asked.

"Acres and acres of tents and mud houses." Sahay's voice was harsh. "I dreamed of a fine place. This is only a place where we might get some water and food, and have a grass roof to keep our heads dry—if it ever rains."

They started down the hill. Rahel thought about Jerusalem. Was it only a dream? No, the elders had said if they walked through the Sudan, they would get to Jerusalem. But could *this* be Jerusalem? The children of Israel—far away from the homeland of Egypt, out in the desert heat—had become angry with Moses. "Have you brought us out into the desert to *die*?" they had shouted. But Moses struck a rock to find water for the people. And hadn't he found manna for them to eat?

Sahay's thin shoulder rippled under Rahel's hand. She had wanted to weep with Sahay in the ravine—poor Sahay, who had lost almost everything. But when Dawit had told her that Sahay would be her new guide, she had also remembered how this girl had spit out the water Dawit gave her and the sound of disgust Sahay had made as she dropped Rahel's hand in the ravine. "I don't want to go with her. She doesn't like me," Rahel had said.

"Someone in our family must make *aliyah*," Dawit had whispered. "It's up to you, now. I'm going to escape again as soon as I can."

"Can't my guide be someone else from our village?"

"I told you that three were killed in the gunfire. The others are young men and have to turn back with me."

Though Rahel was ashamed to admit it, there had been another reason she did not want to put her hand on Sahay's shoulder. Being so close to Sahay made her imagine Sahay's loss, and when she thought of the terrible story Sahay had told her, she became more afraid for Grandmother and the others.

"*Ayezosh*," she whispered to herself. *Sara had probably been filled with longing for home sometimes. And Hirute.* She curled her fingers around the beads, and suddenly felt washed with hope. Perhaps this truly was Jerusalem, now, and her family would soon join her here.

"I wonder how we will find other Falasha people for you to go with when we get into that forest of tents," Sahay said.

Rahel thought about the question she had asked Dawit so long ago. How would she recognize the other Beta-Israel? Her stomach filled with the memories of faces and voices. "At home, I always knew my own people. I knew them all my life."

Sahay didn't say anything, and, for a moment, Rahel wondered what it would be like to be without the other girl's voice, the shoulder under her hand. Then Sahay said, "My aunts and mother showed me the Falasha people at the *markato*. Others I could recognize because of the pottery or blacksmith equipment in front of their houses. That won't help here. Perhaps there's some secret way to tell when you look at a Falasha. But I don't suppose you'd know it."

"I haven't always been blind," Rahel said sharply. "The eye sickness came when I was already old enough to help my mother and grandmother make *injera* and do other work." The smell of new and old graves was growing stronger as they grew nearer. *No, this could not be Jerusalem.*

"Probably there is no secret way, anyway," Sahay said. "Once, my oldest aunt was very sick and had to go to the hospital in Gondar. She told me that the women in her ward discovered a Falasha woman had been staying with them for three days. My aunt said she could not sleep at night after that."

Rahel bit her lower lip. If only she could let go of Sahay's shoulder and fly to Jerusalem. "I think your people look just like my people," she said coldly. "My brother Dawit told me that your people and my people are both part of the Agau who lived in Ethiopia even before the Amhara. Even the storytellers don't remember that long ago."

But Sahay seemed not to notice her anger. "We are coming up to the camp, now," she said.

Rahel listened to the babble of voices. Oh well. Soon she would be with her own people, away from this annoying girl. "Tell me what you see," she said.

The camp, Sahay said, was huge—more people than she had ever seen, surely more than even in Addis Ababa. "I see small mud houses and tents. There are sick people on straw mats. Dust covers everything." Sahay stopped, and Rahel heard the sound of water being poured into barrels, the sound of running feet. The sound made the thirst rise up in her throat. *"Aii,"* Sahay said. "Can't you just taste that water?

But people with jugs and cans are rushing up, and the barrels will be empty in a minute."

Rahel's tongue felt big in her dry mouth. She wanted to catch one of the people rushing by and say, "Water. Water."

"There's a house with a strange roof that is shiny in the sun," Sahay said. "Old women sit in the shade of the roof, looking as if the heat has put them to sleep. Let's go over there and find out where we can get water and food."

Rahel followed Sahay and crouched when she did. She pulled her *shamma* over her head to keep the sun from beating on her, imagining the women, all with their white *shammas* pulled up over their heads.

"The water comes once a day," a woman said, in answer to Sahay's questions. "And there is some food. The white *ferenjis* give it out. But there is never enough."

"Swedish *ferenjis*," another woman said.

"*Ferenjis* are *ferenjis*." Rahel heard someone scratch with a stick in the dust. "Look—there's one of them."

"What does the *ferenji* look like?" Rahel whispered to Sahay.

"Her hair is the color of dried grass. And her skin . . . I wonder how it came to be such a strange color."

Rahel touched the beads until she found the right

one. "Here's what my grandmother told me: God made people by taking a batch of clay and baking it. The first batch of clay was taken from the fire too soon. Those underbaked people became the white races. Then God took some more clay, but this batch burned. Those became very black people, like the Sudanese. Only the third batch was just right. Those people were put in Ethiopia, close to the heart of God."

Sahay sighed. "Now that I've been in this heat, I know the highlands of Ethiopia were close to the heart of God. Well, let's walk. I wonder if I will find any Kemant here."

As she got to her feet, Rahel thought about the story she had just told. She had asked Dawit, as they walked down the mountains, "Was it only Beta-Israel who were put close to the heart of God?" He had answered, "I don't know. I learned in high school that there are many Agau groups, to say nothing of the Amhara and others in Ethiopia. Kemant and Kwara and Beta-Israel are all part of the Agau people who live west of the Tekeze and north of Lake Tana—practically brothers." He laughed a bitter laugh. "Brothers like Cain and Abel."

The babble of voices beat on Rahel's ears. Sahay stopped and greeted a woman. "Can you tell me if most of the people in this camp are Amhara?"

"Amhara, Oromo, Tigre," the woman answered. "The old divisions do not matter so much here."

"Except for the Falashas, of course," a man's voice added. "We all know the Falashas brought most of the troubles that came upon Ethiopia—famine, sickness, everything."

Brothers like Cain and Abel, Rahel thought bitterly. *So, it is no different here.*

"And there is even more sickness here than back in Ethiopia," the first woman continued. "One Swedish *ferenji* nurse works with the sick. There are also two or three Ethiopian nurses who were trained before they fled from Ethiopia, like all the rest of us. But what can a few nurses do against the flood of sickness?"

"Too many sick," another agreed. Rahel heard the murmurs. "Hunger. Measles. Malaria."

Does the malaria come as a tall, thin woman at midnight? Rahel wondered. She would have to ask Sahay to keep her eyes ready for such a woman. Rahel listened to the talking. *At least,* she reminded herself, *there would be a little water here, even if Moses didn't appear to strike a rock.*

Suddenly, she felt a woman's hand on her arm. "Many, many people come into this camp," the woman said. She clicked her tongue. "But take care, children, take care. Many of the people who come in do not live to see the outside of Umm Rekuba."

▲ ▼ ▲ ▼ ▲ ▼ ▲ ▼ ▲ ▼ ▲ ▼ ▲ ▼ ▲

The Falashas

Rahel felt something crawling on her leg, near her foot. When she reached down, she realized it was only sweat. The piercing sun was everywhere, and no escaping it. Even draping her *shamma* over her head did not keep it off. She took her hand from Sahay's shoulder. It didn't matter if the other girl walked on. She was in the middle of a river of people. Someone could help her find the Beta-Israel.

Rahel untied her bag, took out her flute, and played a *tezzeta*—the music of longing for home. Into the song, she put all of her sadness and fear. What was happening to the men who had been turned back? Had they been put in prison, where they would be beaten on the feet until they couldn't walk? Had they been taken to the war, never to return? Dawit told her that the young men who were taken from the village by soldiers were put in the front of the army, so they would die first. Dawit had known they would be coming for him soon. He was the one who should have escaped, but she was the one who had.

Where was Grandmother? Was she walking, even now? Could she walk all the many, many footsteps it had taken to get here? Down the steep places, hugging the cliff? Through the burning heat? When they reached this place, would Grandmother find her? Would she know what to do about *aliyah*? Or would she sit, dazed, as Sahay said other old women did? Rahel let the music die away, let the hand with the flute in it drop to her side.

She heard Sahay asking if anyone knew of other Kemant. Sahay did not ask about Falashas, probably because she was afraid of what people might say to this question.

No one Sahay asked knew anything about the Kemant, but they talked about Falashas. "They could be right here among us," a woman whispered to Sahay. "There's no way to tell anymore. Some even tattoo crosses onto their foreheads so they will look Christian."

"Back in Ethiopia, they could bring corpses back to life to work in the fields for them," someone else said.

As Rahel listened, she fingered the beads. Which was the story for this camp? Maybe the one about the Queen of Sheba, who left Ethiopia to go on a long journey, crossing the Red Sea to stand in Jerusalem before King Solomon and test his great wisdom. The

Queen of Sheba had survived her hard trip, and all the Amhara kings had later been descendants of the son of the Queen of Sheba and King Solomon. No, maybe the story was still the Exodus, the wandering for forty years. How many years would she have to wait in the desert before her family came?

Suddenly, Rahel was impatient. She needed to get to the place where the other Beta-Israel stayed. How had she walked so long among strangers? Before this trip, no one in her family had eaten food prepared by someone who was not Beta-Israel. Grandmother had even told her of a time when people had to go through a cleansing ceremony after any contact with someone who was not Beta-Israel.

Rahel listened for the words she needed. Before long, she found them. "Most of the Falashas live together," someone told Sahay, "in the worst part of the camp."

Rahel reached out and tugged Sahay's arm. "Take me there," she said. "Among my people, some will help me."

To Rahel's surprise, Sahay's voice was sharp. "Where were your people when you needed someone to lead you to Umm Rekuba?"

Rahel frowned. Why should Sahay be angry? They had both survived the long walk. Now they could find places where they really belonged.

▲ ▼ ▲ ▼ ▲ ▼ ▲ ▼ ▲ ▼ ▲ ▼ ▲ ▼ ▲

Despair

Is the smell and heat of the camp already making me crazy? Sahay wondered. Why had she felt this sudden desolation, first when Rahel took her hand away from Sahay's shoulder and now even more strongly? She should have been angry at the Falasha girl for ordering her around, but that was not the feeling sitting in her stomach. *Yes, it must be craziness.* "Forget what I said," she told Rahel.

It was easy to find her way to the worst part of the camp, to the houses where the Falashas stayed. Sahay saw that each small house had so many people that almost all the spaces were filled up.

What the people had said about the Falashas just now—that was foolishness. Once she might have believed it. Now that she, herself, had felt the stones of frightened children, heard them calling her a *buda*, she saw how people could get caught up in such talk.

She helped Rahel find a little shade under a small acacia tree. Rahel sat with her flute in her lap, clutching a small bag in one hand.

Then Sahay stood and flipped her *shamma* back over her shoulder. Flies buzzed around their faces. Rahel's face was shiny in the heat. *Who will be Rahel's eyes for her?* Sahay wondered. The people sitting outside their houses looked too weak to care. But Sahay was glad she did not have to live here among the Falashas, where people might think she was Falasha, too. Rahel would have to find help on her own.

"May you be well," Sahay said. "I hope your brother comes for you."

"May you be well."

The smell of dust was everywhere as Sahay turned away. The rest of the day, she wandered from group to group, asking what region people had come from, looking for any faces she might have seen in the houses that were scattered along the footpaths near her house—or in the sacred groves where the Kemant gathered. But there were none. Finally, she simply found a house with an empty mat, lay down, and covered her face with her *shamma*.

Sahay had found her way to shelter, but she almost wished she had died along the way. Sadness clung to her the way smoke from the cook fire at home clung to her clothes.

▲ ▼ ▲

In the ten days that followed, Sahay felt too hot and weak to talk to anyone, too hot to do anything except sit in shade and try to keep away from the sickness that was everywhere. Although she did not starve, there was never enough to eat. In the morning, before it became too hot, she dragged herself to the edge of the camp and watched for her uncle's face among the people who got off the trucks or came limping into the camp. But he never came. Without intending to, she also looked for Rahel's brother, but he was never there, either.

One morning, she felt too drained even to go to the edge of the camp. She just sat looking down at her lap. Dust had turned her hands the color of ashes. Mud, from sweat and dust, was caked on the insides of her elbows and the backs of her knees. Where her legs rested against each other, her skin was so hot it almost burned.

Now that she had no steps to take, one after the other, loneliness for her uncle was eating her. She thought she might be swallowed completely. *What did he think we would do,* she wondered, *when we got to the Sudan?* Probably he didn't know. They had fled to the only shelter they knew. *What would he have done when he found out what Umm Rekuba was? What was there to do?*

Sahay began to tremble. She was about to be snuffed out, after all, from hopelessness. Should she go look for her uncle one more time? Or should she just let herself be snuffed out? No one had hope. People were just doing what they could, just sitting with their children in the feeding station when the children became too weak from hunger to eat.

She got up and groped her way to the edge of the camp, sat down in the shade of a truck, and leaned against one of the big tires. As she watched a group of people straggle up in their torn clothes, she also saw people walking away from the camp, people with their faces set toward Ethiopia. Some people had grown so full of disgust at the sickness and hunger and heat that they were leaving the camp and starting the long journey back to Ethiopia. "Why shouldn't we die in Ethiopia with all the members of our family," they said, "rather than die here?"

Sahay thought about joining a group going back. No, she would never survive another desert trip, and she would never find her uncle there. But her uncle might also never arrive here. She had always looked to the elders in her family to tell her what to do. Now she had no one. All around her were people sitting, waiting, with silent, staring eyes that held no hope. *Waiting, waiting—for what? To die?*

Sahay got up and limped back into camp. All the rest of that day and part of the next, she did not look for her uncle. She did nothing except lie on her mat with her memories.

Her grandmother's wrinkled face looked down at her. She turned the spindle in one hand and twisted the cotton into a long thread with the other. As she worked, she sang. Sahay sang, too, and they tossed the song back and forth to each other as if it were a plaything.

She felt her father's cheek against her cheek and heard his strong voice as he argued with her uncle by the glow of the evening candle. Her mother stooped beside her, guiding her hand, as she learned to pour the batter for the *arah* onto the black, clay griddle and to watch the bubbles that appeared in the *arah* to show it was ready to eat. In the stream, the water was cold around her ankles. Over and over she saw her cousin Waldu, prancing, laughing, kicking the clay pot. If only she had some of that water now.

Sahay remembered the trip, too—her uncle's face floating over her after the children threw stones at her. The chewy, yellow taste of the corn. The feel of Rahel's hand on her shoulder.

In the evening of that second day, Sahay got up from her mat and began to wander slowly around the camp. Whatever Rahel was doing now, she was lucky that she could not see Umm Rekuba. Old people and young people, both, lay on their mats with thin sticks for arms and legs. She saw a baby on its mother's lap, and she saw in its eyes that it would not be alive through the night.

A great sadness poured over her like water. All the water she thought had dried up in the desert heat now ran down her cheeks and into the dust. She was crying for the baby that would be dead by morning. She was crying for her mother and father and grandmother and cousins, for her mountain home and her uncle. By the time she had finished crying, she felt just a trickle of the old stubbornness in her stomach. If her uncle was not here to make decisions for her, she would make them for herself. And the first thing she would do was go find Rahel, who at least shared the journey with her. *When you have nobody,* Sahay thought, *even a blind Falasha girl is somebody.*

As she approached the Falasha part of the camp, she began to study each face. Everywhere she looked, men and women huddled on the hard ground, their gray-white *shammas* pulled over their heads. No Rahel. A feeling of panic rippled through her. Was Rahel one of the many dead?

No. Sahay's shoulders sagged with relief. There she was—sitting under the same acacia tree where Sahay had left her. While Sahay watched, Rahel groped for her flute and put it to her lips, playing a few soft notes. She looked even thinner than when they had gotten to the camp, and Sahay wondered if anyone was making sure she got her portion of food.

Sahay walked over to Rahel, bent down, and kissed her on both cheeks. For days she had touched no one, and the other girl's face felt like the sun-warmed earth of the fields back in Ethiopia. "You have no family," Sahay said. "And neither do I. I want to stay with you in the Falasha part of the camp."

Rahel pulled her *shamma* up and covered her face, saying nothing. Then she said, "You don't belong here."

"I know." Sahay sat down. If she sat here, how could Rahel chase her away? After a while, when Rahel had said nothing more, Sahay said, "Do you still think about Jerusalem?"

Rahel rubbed her cheek, which was gray with dust. "The children of Israel had to live through ten plagues before Moses led them out," she said. "Maybe this is our time of plagues before the *aliyah*, the going to Israel."

Sahay took Rahel's hand, remembering another time she had held this hand. "You have hope," she whispered.

Rahel said nothing, but her face softened a little.

"I've been thinking about home," Sahay said. "I've been thinking of my grandmother, teaching me to spin."

"My grandmother taught me to spin, too," Rahel said.

"I dreamed that I was eating *arah* and *saweh* with my family again."

"Why do you call it that?"

Sahay thought. "I know the Amharic words: *wat* and *injera*. But food is something we still call in the old words. The Kemant words."

Rahel was quiet. Then she said, "You must have found none of your people here. I'm sorry."

"Let me stay with you," Sahay said again. "I can take you to the edge of the camp every day, and we will try to find my uncle and your brother."

Rahel blew a few notes on the flute. Then she said, "You mustn't say *Falasha,* then. We are Beta-Israel. The House of Israel."

"Beta-Israel." The words felt strange in Sahay's mouth. But she thought that she could at least try to remember to say them. That night, she crowded into the little house Rahel lived in with thirteen women and a few children. And, the next day, they made their first trip together to the edge of the camp. "Do you think it's possible they will never come?" Sahay asked as she watched an old man limp in.

Rahel's face was set in stubbornness, and she didn't reply; so Sahay didn't ask again.

When they were back under the tree, Rahel said, "Tell me what you see. Any sign that the *aliyah* is starting?"

Sahay looked around. "I see only hungry people. A woman not too far from here is shaking with sickness, and other women are standing around her."

Rahel gave a soft sigh. "We have to guard the sick people, so when they die they can be buried early in the morning or late at night in the right way."

A few minutes later, the women began the wailing sound of mourning. Sahay shivered. "Do you think one of us will be the next to die?"

"The elders said the way would be hard," Rahel

said thoughtfully. "Let me tell you the story I've been thinking about." She began:

Suryal, the Angel of Death, came and said, "Moses, I am the one tasted by women and children, the one who destroys houses and builds graves until the coming of the end of the world." But Moses asked Suryal for a few more hours to say farewell to his family. So Suryal sat shaded from the sun and waited. Moses wept as he said good-bye to his wife and children. Suddenly God appeared. "Why do you weep?" God asked. Moses said he was afraid for his wife and his children. So God gave Moses strength to smite the sea, and, from the depths of the sea, a stone cracked apart. In the stone was a small worm eating grass. "Blessed be God who did not forget me, even while I was in the depths of the sea," said the worm. Then Moses understood that if God did not forget a worm in the depths of the sea, God would not forget Moses' wife and children. "I'm ready to meet Suryal, now," Moses told God, and they walked together to where Suryal still sat, waiting.

"When the Kemant talk about Moses," Sahay said, "we say Moses hid the truth from God one time and so Moses vanished."

"That's not true."

"It's what my grandmother told me."

Rahel held her mouth tightly closed and wouldn't talk. So Sahay didn't talk, either. But after a while, she was sorry and missed the sound of their voices, so she said, "My grandmother also said things about Abraham. She would say, 'Let your house be as Abraham's house, and let God make you as prosperous as Abraham was.' "

Rahel's face was still stubborn. "What about Yehudit?"

Sahay thought. In the Tigrean language, where *gudit* means evil, she had heard schoolchildren say, "Yehudit the Gudit." But Rahel would hate to hear such a thing. And who knew if that was even true? "In the language of our prayers," she said, "*yehudit* means very beautiful. I would like to have seen her ride into Axum."

Rahel smiled. "Yes. I would, too."

▲ ▼ ▲ ▼ ▲ ▼ ▲ ▼ ▲ ▼ ▲ ▼ ▲ ▼ ▲ ▼ ▲ ▼

PART 5

Making Aliyah

▲ ▼ ▲ ▼ ▲ ▼ ▲ ▼ ▲ ▼ ▲ ▼ ▲ ▼ ▲ ▼ ▲

The Secret

Every day, after they made their trip to the edge of the camp, Sahay and Rahel sat under the acacia tree. Rahel would play her flute, and Sahay would hold Rahel's bag of Ethiopian dirt in her hands and dream of the highlands, of kites swimming in the air, of blue flax and yellow *maskal* daisies.

"Your songs and stories are my only comfort," Sahay said one day. "I would like to tell you a story." Because of Rahel's flute, Sahay thought the best one to tell would be the story of Yared. Sahay had always liked Yared. Her family always said she was like him: stubborn. Yared had so much trouble with his studies, Grandfather had said, that one day, to escape them, he ran out into the trees where he sat watching a caterpillar climb a tree and fall, climb and fall, climb and fall. The caterpillar taught Yared not to give up, and Yared became a great musician.

"Once," Sahay began, "when Yared was singing

and dancing before Emperor Gabra Maskal, the king was so full of the beautiful music that he did not know what he was doing and let his spear stab Yared's foot. Yared, too, was so full of the music that he didn't even notice the spear. The king was so moved by Yared's love of music, he said he would grant Yared anything he wanted. Yared said he wanted to leave the court and live all alone, where the doves brought music to his ear from God."

Rahel put her hand to the amber beads that hung around her neck. "We tell that story, too," she said. "Some of the elders say that Yared's mother was Beta-Israel."

Sahay frowned. *Could that possibly be true? Well, what did it matter anymore?* She was surprised at how many things she and Rahel had in common—not only the Sabbath but other feast days. And when they prayed, they both faced Jerusalem. "Perhaps God really did bake your people and my people in the same batch," she said. "We seem to know many of the same stories. But there is a big difference. The Kemant might have talked about visiting Jerusalem, but I never heard anyone say we would live there some day."

"Our elders always told us that we came to Ethiopia through the Sudan long ago and someday we would return to Jerusalem through the Sudan," Rahel said. "Some people here have told me we will make *aliyah* from Umm Rekuba."

"Yes," Sahay said scornfully. "And our elders told us that Falashas can turn themselves into hyenas."

Rahel laughed. "Sometimes you remind me of my grandmother. Anyway, I wish I could turn myself into a hyena. I would take us far away from here."

Sahay idly scratched a white line down the dry skin of her arm with an acacia thorn. Yes, if only there were a way to go far from Umm Rekuba. What was here? Every day, they looked for her uncle and Dawit among the faces of the new people who crowded into the camp, but still she had never seen them or anyone else she knew. "I'll see if I can find us some food," she said.

Rahel wouldn't eat the kind of oil the camp gave out. Usually, Sahay traded the oil for chickpeas, which they roasted and ate one by one. Some of the Falasha people had stopped eating altogether because, they said, the Sudanese camp director was trying to poison everyone.

As Sahay walked away from Rahel, she could hear the sound of the flute following her. How could it have happened, she wondered with a small smile, that a Falasha girl had become as precious as water?

On the way back, she could hear the sound of the flute floating toward her from a long way off. This time the music was not like the music Rahel usually made. It sounded as if the time had come for a day of great feasting after everyone had survived the long fast.

Sahay hurried back to the tree. At the sound of footsteps, Rahel stopped playing and looked up, smiling. Her little bag was tied beside her on the ground. "Kneel down," she whispered. "I must tell you a secret."

Sahay put down the food and knelt in the dust, but she wanted to put her hands over her ears to keep out Rahel's words. She knew in her stomach she would not be happy with this secret Rahel had to tell her.

"Aliyah," Rahel whispered. "I told you it would come."

Sahay pulled back. "What are you saying?"

"Come close." Rahel's voice was impatient. "No one else must hear what I have to say. You know everybody would like to leave Umm Rekuba, but most people have no place to go. If the secret spreads, people will be very angry."

Sahay bent close again, and Rahel said in a quiet, quiet voice, "While you were gone, a man came and whispered in my ear. Tonight when the people are sleeping, someone will tap on the mud wall outside. The person who taps will know the way to a secret place where a truck is waiting. The Beta-Israel are going to Jerusalem. And the orphans, the sick, and the old are to go first."

Sahay moved back and stared at her. Surely this could not be true. Jerusalem was no more real than her dreams of fine cloth and a place where she would never have to carry water.

She did not know what to say. But she saw in Rahel's face that Rahel believed what the man had said. Could it be true? Was she to lose Rahel as she had lost everyone else?

Anger churned in Sahay's stomach and beat on her head. She wanted to run through the camp and shout the secret out loud. Someone would stop the *aliyah*. The camp director should not allow *aliyah*. She wrapped her arms around her stomach and rocked back and forth. For the second time since she had come to the camp, the tears ran down her face and wet the *shamma* around her neck.

She was careful not to make a noise, but Rahel somehow knew. *"Ayezosh,"* Rahel said. Sahay looked at her—a ragged blind Falasha girl would be one of the first to leave this camp for a better life. But why not? It was said, "Better a live farmer than a dead king." Why should Rahel stay and die in this camp?

The anger left Sahay's stomach as quickly as it had come. She might as well shout at her poor mother and father, who had also left her, as shout at Rahel. "Spend the night well," Sahay said. "I hope your journey gives you peace." Everything inside of her felt like a clay pot that had suddenly been knocked against a stone and broken to bits.

▲ ▼ ▲ ▼ ▲ ▼ ▲ ▼ ▲ ▼ ▲ ▼ ▲ ▼ ▲

Silver Fish

Rahel wiped the sweat from her face with one corner of her *shamma*. She reached out and touched Sahay's arm. "But you're coming, too. I gave the man your name."

Rahel felt Sahay's *shamma* brush her arm as Sahay settled beside her and put some chickpeas in her hand. For a few minutes, the crunching of chickpeas was the only sound. Finally, Sahay spoke. "What are you talking about? I'm not Beta-Israel."

"I know. But how could I find my way without you? I told him you were my sister." Rahel touched the side of Sahay's face. "Once you saved my life. Now perhaps I can save yours." She lifted her flute and played the joyful song again.

After Rahel had finished, she sat silently, waiting for Sahay to speak. How strange she had felt as she had whispered to the man about Sahay. How strange and hard this *aliyah* was after all. But if Hirute, who was a stranger and not even one of the children of Israel, could follow Nahomey and become an ancestor of the great King Dawit and King Solomon, why couldn't Sahay go to Jerusalem?

"The Kemant," Sahay finally said, "knowing all the things that can happen to a person's family, have ways for people to make new kin, not of one's own blood. People who are sisters and brothers by choice, not by kinship, are *mahala*. *Mahala* do special things for each other and talk about things they would never talk about with other people. They call each other by special names. So perhaps what you told the man is not a complete lie." Her breath caught. "Do you really think he will take me if I decide to go?"

"I think perhaps you are like Hirute," Rahel said.

"Tell me," Sahay said.

After Rahel was done with the story, she ate her dried peas. Who could know how long the road might be to Jerusalem? Perhaps it would be long and thirsty and full of terror, as the road out of Ethiopia had been. She would have to remember she was traveling in the footsteps of the Queen of Sheba and use the queen's story to keep her strong.

That night, like so many nights, Rahel and Sahay lay down in the crowded hut to sleep. But Sahay tossed like branches in a wind.

"What's wrong?" Rahel whispered.

"What if my uncle comes when I'm gone? He would think I was dead . . . and could I bring such sadness to him? I must stay here and wait for him."

Rahel thought of Grandmother's voice in the *tukul,* so long ago, comforting her. She wanted to find words to comfort Sahay, but what could they be?

Slowly, Rahel began to talk, forming each word carefully. "Sahay, I am afraid for my family, too. Here, other Beta-Israel have told me horrible stories, stories of whole villages killed. And you know how hard the road is." She swallowed. "Once, you told me your uncle said, 'You must carry the future with you.' What kind of future is there in Umm Rekuba? You and I will die here. Even Moses did not want to die. Won't you come with me and fulfill the dreams your uncle had for you?"

Sahay didn't answer. Rahel lay still in the quiet and stared upward, remembering that night she had left her home, remembering the feel of her family's kisses. On that night, her words had changed her grandmother's mind. Would they change Sahay's, too? Or would she lose Sahay and once more have to set off carrying her loss on her back? She listened to her sadness, but it said nothing, only wound itself tightly in her stomach.

When Rahel heard the tap on the mud wall of the house, she picked up her bag and stood up silently. If

Sahay wasn't coming, she would still have to find a way, even if she had to walk with loneliness rattling inside her, *chrrr, chrrr*. She turned to grope her way to the door. Then she heard a rustling. "I still don't know if I should go," Sahay whispered sadly. "But you're right. Even Moses did not want to die. All I can do for my uncle now is keep refusing to be snuffed out."

"How great is my joy," Rahel whispered. With her hand on Sahay's shoulder, Rahel stooped from the house.

As they walked, Rahel thought about the great camp and the people moaning on their mats, people with nowhere to go. She thought about Sahay. Rahel's own family might find her in Jerusalem, but Sahay was leaving behind her only chance to see her uncle again. Pity and sadness rose up in a wave and she thought of one of the last stories Grandmother had given her, a story about judgment day. "God will change the heaven and earth like clothing. The angel Michael, with eyes like doves and a robe of lightning, will blow the trumpet on Mount Sinai. The angels will bring two oxen, one from the east, one from the west; the name of the first is Grace and the name of the other is Pity." In the most terrible of times, were grace and pity the only things left?

Rahel heard the man stop to tap on other walls, and other footsteps joined theirs. The group limped silently through the camp and out into the desert, out where the whirring of insects was the only sound—*with only the stars and grass to see us,* Rahel thought.

When they were far from Umm Rekuba, Rahel whispered to Sahay, "Now we are walking again with a guide. I hope this walk will be a happier one." Though she was hungrier and weaker than she had been on the first walk, knowing that she was walking toward Jerusalem made her feel she could walk on and on if she must.

This time, thanks be to God, they did not have to walk far. After some minutes, Sahay stopped. "What is it?" Rahel asked.

"A truck, like a large rock in the grass."

Rahel had never been in a truck before. Inside, she squeezed into a corner. The truck started, rattling her teeth against one another.

"I wish my brother were here to see the *aliyah,*" she whispered. "My grandmother told us over and over about this day."

"I wish my uncle were here," Sahay whispered back.

Rahel took Sahay's hand, feeling again the great sadness and the great excitement of the first night of leaving. Tears dropped onto her fingers. When Rahel felt them, she said, "*Ayezosh.* My family and your uncle may get out. Until they do, we carry their hope." Sahay didn't reply, but she squeezed Rahel's hand.

The truck went and went, taking them far from Umm Rekuba. When it stopped, Rahel felt as if her bones had been rattled. "Quickly," voices outside the truck said. "Quickly, quickly." Hands took hold of Rahel and helped her out of the truck, pushed her forward onto ground that was hard and smooth under her feet.

Once again, they walked, this time across the hard, smooth earth. "There is a great silver fish ahead of us," Sahay said, "and people are climbing up into its belly. I think it will be easier to climb than the mountains of Ethiopia, though."

Making *aliyah*! Rahel started up and up into the belly of the fish. At the top, hands guided her in and helped her find a seat on the hard floor. She could hear the sounds of more and more people crowding in. "Every space on the floor is filled," Sahay whispered. An old man groaned, and Rahel heard his family comfort him.

"Where are we?" she asked. "Is this Jerusalem?"

"I don't know," Sahay said. She took Rahel's hand and rubbed it along the floor. "Does this feel like Jerusalem?" she asked. "What did your elders tell you?"

Rahel tried to think. She couldn't remember the elders saying anything about a giant fish.

"Sit still. Sit still," a woman called to everyone. Suddenly, the fish began to move. With a roar like a flooding river, it rushed through the night, faster than the fastest animal, and lurched upward. Rahel grabbed her stomach and closed her eyes.

As she opened them again, she smelled the strong warm smell of coffee. *"Buna,"* she said to Sahay. How long ago had her mother roasted coffee beans over the fire and then pounded them to make hot coffee?

"People are passing it in cups," Sahay said. "Are we in Jerusalem?"

"Soon," a woman in a soldier's uniform said. "You are flying to Jerusalem."

Flying? Rahel slurped the coffee, remembering the sound of the iron bird high above the *markato.* Grandmother said the iron bird rained fire.

"My cousins and I used to talk about these birds," Sahay said. "Where they came from and what kind of animal they might be, or if they were animal at all."

So, Rahel thought, *we are not in the belly of a fish but one of the iron birds.* Would they be rained down onto Jerusalem like fire, then? If so, it would be even more exciting than the Queen of Sheba, who only got to ride in on a camel. She took the little bag of dirt from the bag at her waist and held it to her nose to drink in the smell. *Oh Grandmother. If only you could see me making this new* aliyah *story.*

▲ ▼ ▲ ▼ ▲ ▼ ▲ ▼ ▲ ▼ ▲ ▼ ▲ ▼ ▲

Jerusalem

The *buna* was hot and sweet, and, as Sahay drank, the warmth came into her mouth and throat. But she was not warmed in her stomach. Everything trembled in the belly of the iron bird. She was sure her strength had gone away for the last time, leaving only the Red Terror.

What was she doing going to a Falasha land? Would people be able to tell, when they looked at her, that she did not belong in Jerusalem? What would happen to her in a place she did not belong when the iron bird spit them out? A person far from his own country, the Kemant said, was like a horse that always had to wear a bridle. Even with the warm *buna,* she began to shake and could not stop.

"What's the matter?" Rahel whispered.

"I don't know," Sahay whispered back. She hadn't wanted to stay in Umm Rekuba. But she didn't want to go to Jerusalem either. She was going as

Rahel's sister, and she didn't really want to have a Falasha as a *mahala*. But what choice did she have? "Perhaps I have the shaking sickness," she said. "Perhaps I will be dead before we see Jerusalem."

If Rahel answered, Sahay did not hear her. The woman in a soldier's uniform brought a blanket and Sahay put it all the way over her head, but still she shook. Would Jerusalem be a place of mountains and cool winds? *Maybe it's better,* she thought, *to die here. Why should I go to a country with no Kemant, a place where I will have to live always surrounded by strangers?* Sahay closed her eyes, under the blanket, and let the sleep come over her.

Many hours later, she was awakened by Rahel's hands grabbing her. Noise was everywhere, and she felt as if they were being swept away in a rushing river filled with rains. "Tell me what is happening," Rahel said.

Sahay pushed the blanket back. "I think we are dying." It was hard to talk because of the noise and her shaking. "We are both dying."

Rahel hardly moved. "At least we will die going to Jerusalem," she said. "And if I see Suryal coming toward me, I will remember the small worm eating grass at the bottom of the sea."

Sahay stared at her. Rahel was just a girl, a ragged girl who could not see, but she was not afraid. "You have so much courage," she said.

"But Sahay," Rahel said, "you are brave, too.

When I had to leave my brother, you were the river where I drank my courage in the desert. Day after day in Umm Rekuba, you looked for our families. And now you are going with me on the strange path, just the way Hirute did with Nahomey."

The beast that carried them shuddered and then stopped moving. A murmur moved through the people. "Jerusalem."

"No," the woman in the soldier's uniform said. "This is not Jerusalem yet. We are in Belgium, and we will have a short wait here."

Belgium. The word was so strange. Sahay sat silently in the dark, wondering where they were and what would happen next.

When they went up into the sky again Sahay was not so afraid. She had come to understand that the iron bird was the lord of many motors. But her shaking had not completely stopped. Did the iron birds ever fall out of the sky?

She thought about her father and mother and grandmother and cousins, about her uncle, about everything she had left behind. "Rahel," she whispered. "Rahel, I'm not brave. There's one last thing I didn't tell you in the ravine . . . about that day."

She could hear Rahel's breathing. She swallowed. "I heard my mother calling me to the house. But Waldu grabbed my arm, and we hid in the corn. When we heard the first screams in the house, Waldu yelled, 'Come on.' He got up and ran to the house to help. But I . . . I ran the other way. I ran up into the cave. So I lived and they didn't. Now I'm running to safety again, leaving my uncle behind. I'm abandoning him, just the way I did the rest of my family." She ducked back under the blanket, wiping the tears that ran from her eyes.

"Oh, Sahay," Rahel whispered. "You have no choice but to leave. Your uncle would have wanted you to go. Once, my grandmother said perhaps only the strong-willed will survive these times. Your family would be so happy that you survived to carry their hope with you. You are just as stubborn and just as brave as all the people in my favorite stories."

Sahay sighed. Even through the blanket, she could feel Rahel's arm. She leaned against it. "How can you remember so many stories?" She felt Rahel grope under the blanket for her hand.

"This is how," Rahel said. "My grandmother gave me a story to go with each bead."

Sahay felt Rahel's amber beads touch her fingers. She took them with both hands, and her fingers closed on them. The warmth from Rahel's skin comforted her.

On this journey, the iron bird did not fall out of the sky. After a long time, it swooped down and brought them safely to the earth. When the roaring noise stopped, two men came through the door. *"Shalom,"* they called out. *"Baruch haba."*

The woman in the soldier's uniform translated. "Peace to you. Blessed be your coming."

"Shalom," Sahay whispered with the others.

"Truly Jerusalem?" an old man asked.

"Truly Jerusalem."

Even women who were too weak to walk by themselves began to trill the joy cry. "Come," Rahel said. She took hold of her little bag and got to her feet. "Come." Her voice was so full of hope that Sahay stopped shaking a little. Perhaps she did not have the shaking sickness. Perhaps she was only filled with fear to see this new land.

"Hold on to my beads for now," Rahel said. "They will help you remember the stories, too."

Sahay's stomach filled with the sweetness of Rahel's words. There would be times of strangeness and pain in this land, too. But when pain came, she would have stories and a friend to hold on to. "Rahel," she said. "You are not my kin sister. But I want you to be my *mahala* sister. According to my custom, we must give each other special names that only we will use."

"May we both have joy together," Rahel said.

I will never use the word Falasha *again,* Sahay thought, *because Rahel is not a stranger to me.* And when she found someone who could talk to them in the language of Jerusalem that the men had spoken at the door, she would ask that person the names for Nahomey and Hirute.

This time, Rahel was the one who led and Sahay was the one who walked behind with her hand on Rahel's shoulder, holding on for strength.

They stepped out the door of the iron bird into the pale light. Sahay stood looking down. On the ground, a little way off, a crowd of people stood staring up at the newcomers. Sahay saw no mountains— only a yellow land with palm trees, something like the Sudan they had left.

"Tell me what you see," Rahel said.

"I have just seen a flag," Sahay said. "And there is a star sewn onto it, the same star my people and your people sew onto their clothes." Some of the Ethiopian people were walking slowly away from the iron bird. Others were kneeling to kiss the ground. An old man took a little earth and put it on his tongue to taste the new land of Jerusalem.

As Sahay described the old man, Rahel suddenly lifted her flute to her mouth. She began to play a song Sahay had never heard her play before. It was the music of Ethiopia, the music of their childhoods—but it was also a new song, the music of a new land. As Sahay listened to the music, she became like the king who forgot himself when Yared played, and the fear and shaking left her body.

"I see people," she said to Rahel. "They're waiting for us to walk down to them. Some are smiling and others are crying, but their faces look glad to hear your music. I think they are glad to see us coming." Rahel's music filled Sahay's mouth and her eyes and her ears, and when she took the first step down, she saw for herself that they had come to a land where for now, no matter what lay ahead, no one was a stranger.

The history of the many ethnic groups in Ethiopia is complex. Although Rahel and Sahay were born into different ethnic traditions, their people are connected by several threads of that history.

The ancient city of Axum was founded in about 500 B.C.E. by people who came across the Red Sea from Arabia, bringing with them their own Semitic language. These immigrants married among some of the Agau people who were already on the Ethiopian plateau and established their kingdom in what is now northern Ethiopia. Periodically they pushed their control southward, until, according to Ethiopian tradition, in the tenth century an Agau princess or queen named Yehudit rose up in rebellion and led the charge that destroyed the Axumite empire.

After the fall of Axum, Ethiopian kings set up their capitals in other places, including Gondar, founded in 1636, and Addis Ababa, founded in 1887. The people of Ethiopia ultimately formed seventy or eighty different ethnic groups, each speaking a different language. But since most of the Ethiopian kings came from the Amhara ethnic group, the language of the Amharas (Amharic) spread throughout Ethiopia as the official state language.

Judaism and Christianity both have deep roots in Ethiopia. According to Ethiopian traditional stories, the Queen of Sheba lived in Ethiopia. In the tenth century B.C.E., the queen crossed the Red Sea to visit King Solomon of Israel and to learn about his wisdom firsthand. When she returned, it is said, she brought the practice of Judaism back to her native land. Later, the son she had with Solomon established Judaism as the primary religion in the kingdom of Axum. Most of the kings of Ethiopia claimed to be descended from this son.

In the fourth century, Christianity came to Ethiopia. The stories from that time say that two Syrian boys were captured from a ship sailing on the Red Sea. One of those boys, after he grew up, became a teacher to the young king of Ethiopia and established the first churches. Christianity soon became the state religion, although the practice of Ethiopian Orthodox Christianity still kept many Jewish elements.

Through the centuries, the state religion of Ethiopia continued to be Orthodox Christianity, but other religions were also practiced, including Islam and Judaism. No one knows the exact beginning of

Rahel's people, the Agau ethnic group that calls itself the Beta-Israel, "House of Israel." Other ethnic groups that considered themselves superior called the Beta-Israel Falasha, meaning "alien stranger," and persecuted them for their Jewish faith. Some experts believe that the persecution began, in the distant past, as a way of exercising control because the Beta-Israel knew the secrets of iron making. This gave them what was believed to be mysterious power and made them seem dangerous.

Sahay's people, the Kemant, are also Agau. The Kemant groups speak different languages from the Beta-Israel and have their own unique blend of beliefs drawn from Christianity, Judaism, and spirit worship. Although the Kemant hold a higher place in the hierarchy of Ethiopian peoples, both the Beta-Israel and the Kemant are often looked down on by the Amhara and other descendants of the immigrants who founded the Axumite kingdom.

In 1974 Haile Selassie, the last Ethiopian king, was overthrown by a military committee. The men who then came to power spoke of freedom for any religious or ethnic group. They gave land to the Beta-Israel, who had never before been allowed to own land. But within a few years after the revolution, religious persecution was even worse than it had been before.

Meanwhile Eritrea, the very northernmost province of Ethiopia, had stepped up its fight for independence. The military government, based in Addis Ababa, fought back, pulling more and more of the country into what had once been a mostly regional war. The Ethiopian army began to draft young men ages sixteen and older. Particularly in northern Ethiopia, the lives of ordinary people began to be affected more and more by the war, famine, and drought.

The pressures were even more intense on the Beta-Israel than on everyone else. The practice of the Jewish religion was forbidden. Hebrew books were taken or burned. Jewish schools and synagogues were closed. People were put in prison and tortured.

Squeezed by the pressures of violence, hunger, and persecution, people from many ethnic groups began to stream toward the Sudan. But for some of the Beta-Israel, there was another reason for leaving. They were responding to quiet messages passed from person to person that it was time to make *aliyah*.

Where were these messages coming from? In the early 1980s Israel developed a number of secret ways to help Ethiopian Jews get from refugee camps in the Sudan to Israel. Officials in the Ethiopian government insisted that this kind of activity must be stopped. But those who had succeeded in getting to Israel continued to find ways to get word back to Beta-Israel villages that the time foretold by the ancient stories had come. In 1984 ten to twelve thousand people left Beta-Israel villages to go to the Sudan.

The terrain of northern Ethiopia is extremely rugged. Depending on where they started out, people walked for periods from as short as two weeks to more than three months. They had to climb high mountain ridges and plunge thousands of feet into valleys before they reached the desert flatlands. They usually reached the Sudan weak from hunger and dehydrated. The stories of Rahel's and Sahay's flights are woven from the details related by real survivors of many such journeys.

At refugee camps like Umm Rekuba in the Sudan, the Beta-Israel died at the rate of fifteen to twenty people a day. Once the word got out about how desperate the situation was, the government of Israel escalated efforts to get more Ethiopian Jews out. Operation Moses, the first in a series of massive airlifts, transported more than sixty-seven hundred people to Israel in just two months of 1984. After the Sudanese government put a stop to Operation Moses, other secret airlifts—including Operation Joshua, Operation Sheba, and Operation Solomon—continued until the military government of Ethiopia was overthrown in 1989. By then at least forty-five thousand Ethiopian Jews had been helped to emigrate.

Once in Israel, some of the Beta-Israel had a chance to tell the stories of their ordeal to the world. In fact, it was in one such account that I first read this sentence: "One blind girl in the group walked all the way to the Sudan with her hand on her brother's shoulder." But the Ethiopian Jews also faced frightening and often difficult times adjusting to a completely new country. Though the pain of the journey and the pains of adjustment were great, many survivors were able to cling to age-old stories from the Bible and from Ethiopian tradition—the stories that Rahel and Sahay also drew strength from—as they learned to make new homes for themselves and for their children.

—J. K.

GLOSSARY

▲ ▼ ▲ ▼ ▲ ▼ ▲ ▼ ▲ ▼ ▲ ▼ ▲ ▼ ▲

Abraham (ah bruh hahm): a Biblical name meaning "father of multitude"; Islamic, Jewish, and Christian traditions all trace their heritage back to "Father Abraham"

Addis Ababa (ah dees ah bah bah): the capital of Ethiopia, literally translated as "new flower"

Adonay (ah doe nye): the Lord

Agau (ah gaw): the ethnic people believed to have populated the Ethiopian highlands before the Kingdom of Axum

aliyah (ah lee yah): the journey back to the homeland of Israel

Amhara (ahm ha rah): the ethnic group from which most of Ethiopia's kings came

ankelba (ahn kel bah): a cloth or leather sack for carrying a baby

arah (ah rah): the Kemant word for *injera*

ayezosh (aye zosh): a comforting word meaning "be strong"

baaltet (ball tet): a wise older woman

bagana (bah gah nah): an Ethiopian instrument, most often with ten strings, usually used to play solemn music

Baruch haba (ba rook hah bah): a greeting meaning "blessed be your coming"

Beta-Israel (beh tah is rye ale): Ethiopian Jews, literally translated as "House of Israel"

buda (boo dah): a person, believed to possess an "evil eye," who causes misfortune

buna (boo nah): coffee

Dawit (dah weet): David, a Biblical name meaning "beloved"; David was Israel's most famous king

Elias (ee lay ahs): Elijah, a Biblical name meaning "the Lord is my king"; Elijah is an Old Testament prophet

emayay (eh my yay): the word for Mom, used affectionately

Falasha (fah lah sha): a word meaning "alien stranger," used by other ethnic groups in Ethiopia to name Ethiopian Jews

Fasika (fah see kah): the Beta-Israel name for the Passover festival

ferenji (fer en jee): foreigner

Gabra Maskal (geh bre mus kul): a sixth-century Ethiopian emperor whose name is literally translated as "servant of the cross"

gahbi (gah bee): a thick cloak made of cotton

gudit (goo dit): a Tigrean expression for evil

Haile Selassie (hye lee sel ah see): the last emperor of Ethiopia (1930–74), whose name is translated as "Might of the Trinity"

Hirute (hee root): Ruth, a Biblical name meaning "delight"; Ruth was a Moabite ancestor of King David

imbi (im bee): a word usually used to indicate that a person or animal is being obstinate

injera (in jeh rah): flat Ethiopian bread; a thin, sourdough pancake

Isahac (ees ah hawk): Isaac, a Biblical name meaning "laughter"; Isaac was Abraham's son

Kemant (keh ment): one of the ethnic divisions of the Agau people

kes (kase): a religious leader

kita (kee tah): an unleavened bread made by the Beta-Israel people

Kwara (kwah rah): one of the ethnic divisions of the Agau people

Magabit (meh gah beet): the time of our month of March

mahala (mah hah lah): a kinship entered into by choice instead of by birth

markato (mar kah toe): market

maskal (mus kul): literally translated as "cross"; *maskal* daisies cover the fields after the time of heavy rains; named after Maskal, the Ethiopian holiday celebrating the finding of the True Cross, which marks the Christian new year in September

Nahase (neh hah sey): the time of our month of August, the Ethiopian twelfth month, usually the time of heaviest rain

Nahomey (nah hoe mey): Naomi, a Biblical name meaning "companion"; Naomi was Ruth's mother-in-law

nug (noog): a seed used for its oil

Oromo (oh roh moh): the largest ethnic group in Ethiopia

Rahel (rah hel): Rachel, a Biblical name meaning "lamb" or "ewe"; Rachel was Jacob's second wife

Sahay (seh hi): there is no English equivalent for this name, which is literally translated as "sun"

Sara (sah rah): Sarah, a Biblical name meaning "princess"; Sarah was Abraham's wife

saweh (saw weh): the Kemant word for *wat*

shamma (shah mah): a light, gauzy cloak made of cotton

shifta (shif tah): a bandit

Suryal (suer yal): the Angel of Death

tazkar (tahz kahr): an ancient religious ritual, part of Kemant, Beta-Israel, and Amhara custom, of holding a second funeral a few months after a person has died, to help make sure the person's soul reaches the supernatural world

Tekemt (teh kempt): the time of our months of October and November, when the crops are harvested

Tewodros (teh drohz): Theodore; a Biblical name meaning "God's gift"; King Tewodros II was the emperor of Ethiopia from 1855–1868

tezzeta (teh zeh tah): a song of longing for a beloved person or a country, literally translated as "remembrance"

Tigre (tih grey): an ethnic group from northern Ethiopia

tukul (too kul): a small, round Ethiopian house

Waldu (wohl du): there is no English equivalent for this name, which is literally translated as "son"

wat (wuht): a spicy stew, frequently the main dish of an Ethiopian dinner

Yakob (yah cob): Jacob, a Biblical name meaning "supplanter"; Jacob was Isaac's son

Yared (yah red): Jared, a Biblical name meaning "descendant"; Jared was a famous Ethiopian musician considered to be the "father" of Ethiopian church music

Yehudit (yeh hoo dit): Judith, a Biblical name meaning "very beautiful" or "praised one"; Judith was an Old Testament heroine

Note: The Amharic language is written in an alphabet very different from our Roman alphabet. When people use the Roman alphabet to write Amharic words, they do a bit of guessing to try to reproduce the Amharic sounds; so you may find variations in the English spellings of Amharic words. Amharic also contains some sounds not found in the English language. One of these sounds is the "explosive k," which is often written as a *q*. (Thus the word *Kemant* is sometimes written *Qemant*.) You can pronounce the "explosive k" as you would an English *k*. Another of these sounds is *ts*, a sound found at the beginning of Sahay's name. (Non-native Amharic speakers often pronounce this as an English *s*.) Amharic does not have any stressed syllables.

—J. K.